The Body of the Soul

LUDMILA ULITSKAYA

The Body
of the Soul

STORIES

Translated from the Russian by
Richard Pevear and Larissa Volokhonsky

A MARGELLOS
WORLD REPUBLIC OF LETTERS BOOK

Yale UNIVERSITY PRESS | NEW HAVEN & LONDON

English translation copyright © 2023 by Richard Pevear and Larissa Volokhonsky.

Originally published as о теле души, copyright © 2019 by Ludmila Ulitskaya and AST Publishing House. Published by arrangement with ELKOST International Literary Agency.

Yale University Press books may be purchased in quantity for educational, business, or promotional use. For information, please e-mail sales.press@yale.edu (U.S. office) or sales@yaleup.co.uk (U.K. office).

Set in Source Serif type by Motto Publishing Services.
Printed in the United States of America.

Library of Congress Control Number: 2023933097
ISBN 978-0-300-27093-8 (paperback : alk. paper)

A catalogue record for this book is available from the British Library.

This paper meets the requirements of ANSI/NISO Z39.48-1992 (Permanence of Paper).

10 9 8 7 6 5 4 3 2 1

Contents

The Body of the Soul

Girlfriends

I Need No Others . . .

IN LIEU OF AN INTRODUCTION

Amazons, my girlfriends, young and old,
in varicolored boots, galoshes, sandals, barefoot,
in a chain dance, singing, carefree, tramlike, noisy,
    sometimes shrieky,
all spinning, leaping, and dancing, some a twist, some a
    quadrille.
The world's dancing is sacred,
and their singing is such that it heals the sick, puts children
    to sleep,
yet it cannot bring back the dead,
though maybe it soon will learn.

How beautiful they all are—the curly ones, their braids
    worn like crowns,
and the ones with heads shaven,
their skulls like shining ivory balls,
or the disheveled, with dreadlocks or with soft, hyacinth-
    like curls,
they are light-footed, one does toe dancing, one is skipping,
yet another in a wheelchair, and her friend follows with a
    three-legged cane, after a stroke.

The young ones are leaping, their breasts firm and sharp,
those whose are big and hanging follow, and their plumlike
    nipples bob up and down, playfully,
the flat-chested ones leap, covering their private parts with
    wreaths of herbs . . .

I love you, my friends, for your gaiety, your fidelity,
for your kindness and generosity
and for the maternal feeling with which
you bend down to the small and the weak, be it a mouse or
    a frog,
and how much more a human child.
Tanka, Zoya, Larisa, three Natashkas, Diana, Irisha,
Katya-Lena, Tamara, Ilana, Kristina, and Hanna-Maria,
Nastya, Katya, Kioko . . . Masha, Masha, of course, I almost
    forgot her, because she left so long ago
that her children have had their own children,
and their grandchildren are now grown up . . .
and the chain dance of those who departed whirls higher,
    just raise your eyes
and you'll see their merry heels, or the flimsy slippers
they put in a coffin, you'll see their snow-white shrouds—
Vera, Katya, and Olya, Tamara, Gayane, Marina, Irina, and
    Natalie . . .

We lived our lives together, bearing all our sorrows in our
    arms,
helping each other to carry suitcases, coffins, and sacks of
    potatoes,
sobbing out on each other's chests all the passions and
    frenzies,
all the infidelities, abortions, betrayals, KGB searches,
    shameful envies.

6

We learned to forgive each other, but first we lured away
  husbands,
and fornicated, and lied, and did such things
that after them we knelt in tears and begged,
and awaited each other's forgiveness and mercy, and
  sisterly gentleness and friendship.

I need no others, I love these ones—flighty, wise,
shameless, seductive, deceitful, beautiful, faithless and
  faithful,
smart ones and also unmitigated fools, who could give
  lessons to the angels in heaven . . .
I need you the way you are—and I myself am the same.

The Dragon and the Phoenix

When there was only one week left, although no one could know it, Zarifa asked Musya to dial a number and dictated the figures straight off.

"You have such an exceptional memory," Musya marveled for the thousandth time. But Zarifa had long been used to this marveling and said quite sternly, "Connect me."

Although Zarifa had a secretary, Musya fulfilled secretarial duties better than any secretary. And her English was better than the secretary's, and certainly better than Zarifa's. As was her Russian, French, and—just recently—even Greek, but now it was of no importance.

Musya dialed a number with an unfamiliar country code, a man answered with a long sing-song "Halloo," and Musya moved the receiver right to Zarifa's ear, so that Zarifa had no need to sit up. She began to speak in Azerbaijani, and her voice ripened with power and gentleness.

Musya had some knowledge of this language, though she did not speak it—she had studied in the Russian school of a once peaceful Armenian-Azerbaijani town, where half the children were Russian and the other half Armenian and Azerbaijani children from the cultivated families of the town, those who understood that to get a good education one had to go to Russia. By the time they finished school the children had almost as good Russian as their teacher Aliev, a Russophile and an ardent Communist. In its historical past this school had been Russian, and also the first girls' school in the whole of Karabakh. The teachers were all choice old ones, like museum pieces. Both teachers and pupils in this school were distinguished by one thing: in the labors of perfecting their knowledge of the language of Pushkin and Tolstoy, the disagreements between Armenians and Azerbaijanis were somehow softened, both being equal in their nonbelonging to the great Russian culture . . . Zarifa had graduated from this school eight years earlier than Musya, and they became acquainted many years later in Moscow.

Their native town in Karabakh had long since been gently but persuasively divided into upper and lower, Armenian and Azerbaijani, parts. Everyone lived in a slightly village way—in the yard, in the street. Mixed marriages were rare, and each time it was a special occasion, an event that caused a big stir among relatives and neighbors. Why the stir? Oh, that was a separate matter . . . For some reason marriages with Russians did not arouse such a ferment of the blood.

Musya listened to the conversation. It seemed that Zarifa was inviting her brother to come; the name of the nearest airport was mentioned. Zarifa also asked her brother to do something, but Musya did not catch what it was; she thought she heard the word *dragon* and did not believe her ears . . . Why *dragon?* At the end of the conversation Zarifa said in Russian, "Come, Saïd. And quickly . . ."

Musya took the phone back. Zarifa forbade her to weep. Both were silent. Musya put her porcelain-white hands on the top of the small bedside hospital table and noiselessly shed tears.

It was nearly two years since this cursed illness struck

Zarifa. First she was treated in Munich; there she had been operated on, then moved to Israel; there had been chemo- and radiotherapy, and now they had moved to Cyprus, where long ago Zarifa had bought a house for summer happiness . . . They decided everything wordlessly, each in her own way: Zarifa fought to the last, and Musya, having lost faith in doctors, got involved with two Armenian sorceresses, el- derly sisters, set entirely in gold from their ears and teeth to their ankles. At night, when Zarifa sent her home to get some sleep, Musya secretly conversed with them by Skype. Hers was not a trivial task—it was not about curing Zarifa but about a complicated exchange of one soul for another. The sisters had sent her some special oil to apply to her feet. The older sister, Margot, told her that such an exchange was pos- sible; they had once dealt with a mother who died instead of her son. The sorcery had worked in an intricate way: the boy survived the deadly blood disease after being treated in Moscow by the academician Vorobyev, and the mother was run over by a tramway and died instantly as soon as her son recovered . . .

Musya had graduated from a pedagogical institute in Moscow, was philologically quite educated, well read, and her memory had obligingly offered her Berlioz from *The Master and Margarita:* the sorcery, the tramway, some oil.

"Such a nice boy he was, went into the army, now he's in prison," said one of the sisters, and the other pulled her up short: "Don't spread gossip . . . Miracles happen, they do!"

For three months things became worse and worse, and the miracle would not happen. Musya made a plan for her- self: if the sorceresses did not help perform the exchange and Zarifa departed, she would follow her. There were no tramways in their little Cyprus town, but there was the sea, which splashed right outside their windows, offering various services; and besides, no one had yet abolished the ancient noose.

Why Zarifa's usual good fortune—oh, how lucky she had been all her life!—turned away from her and wanted to collect at once for everything that had been so generously given in advance was on both their minds. But Zarifa conducted a mental audit, trying to calculate at what point a mistake had been made, while Musya's thoughts mingled with ancient motives, with fire, blood, and water, combining in special proportion, and there was no mistake, but only a disheartening hopelessness.

"Stop sniveling. Better eat—look, Katya has brought dolmas . . ."

Katya had been exported from Moscow and was the best housekeeper in the world. Zarifa loved the best; she knew everything about watches, diamonds, fountain pens, cars. And about people.

At this point Musya finally burst into tears. Zarifa had not been eating for a week, did not touch a thing, only drank a little, and the liquid flowing into the plastic bag was no longer pink, but cruelly red. Again, vague ancient thoughts stirred in Musya's head: blood-soul-life poured out, and the liquid that poured in through the dropper, the physiological solution, was turbid . . . Had it been up to her, she would have given all her blood.

"Eat, and I need to make one more call . . . ," ordered Zarifa. "There's this business . . ."

"What business?" Musya asked anxiously.

Zarifa always liked this foolishly charming quality of hers—a total lack of understanding of the business side of life. And she stroked her friend's silky leg, which happened to be there . . . Not a single hair was to be found on Musya's body. From a young age her grandmother had taught her to rub her body with a pumice stone to an icelike smoothness.

After a long decline Zarifa experienced a sudden upsurge of energy. Her finger again pointed to the telephone:

"Call Zhenka Raikhman, tell her to come for the farewell . . ."

"What is it . . . what is it you're saying . . . what farewell . . . ?"

"Tell her whatever you like, but let her come . . . Katya will stay with me tonight, you haven't slept for three nights, go and rest. Come back for dinner, and send Katya to me here by eleven . . ."

They were married twelve years earlier, in Amsterdam. Zarifa had nursed this plan for a long time and was well prepared: she obtained a residence permit in Holland, opened a branch of her firm there, finally bought a cozy house in Amsterdam on the bank of the Amstel River, two steps away from the theater De Kleine Komedie.

After all these preliminary actions, in which matrimonial plans were well combined with business, Zarifa proposed to Musya. They had been living together for five years, but now Musya became frightened. First she had already had one unhappy marriage, from which she had escaped as one escapes from prison, and had then spent a long time purging her memory of the man with prickly stubble and sadistic inclinations.

She swore at the time never again to have any dealings with men, and never to marry, but she did not know where this oath would lead her. It led her into Zarifa's arms. Second, which was in fact "first": it was terrifying to announce to the whole world that she was . . . To this day the word *lesbian* made Musya freeze, like a little girl caught stealing. Terror was lurking at the deepest depth of her timid soul; she knew that it was bad—her mother almost lost her mind when she found out about Zarifa, and forbade her to tell it to the relatives . . . And now Zarifa proposed marriage! To decline? Impossible. Everything Zarifa did was superlative: she was a successful lawyer, the best negotiator, and an excellent businesswoman, and as a person she was both able to take risks and at the same time cautiously provident. Musya was proud of Zarifa: she could do everything, absolutely everything—skydive, speed drive; in her younger years she was good at playing Preference; recently she gambled on occasion at the casino and never lost! . . .

Musya kept trying to stop Zarifa's brave follies. But her timid entreaties always ended in the same way: resolute, unfeminine tenderness and energetic caresses. Zarifa was extremely moved by Musya's—maternal or childish—fearful anxiety, her constant superstitious worry about her.

The marriage certificate issued by the administration of the most tolerant city in the world, set in a frame of stamped white velvet, now hung on the wall of the drawing room of their Cyprus house. When this certificate was first shown to Zhenka Raikhman, she clowningly kissed the piece of paper and said, "You girls used to be nothing but whores, and now you're respectable spouses"—and they all burst out laughing.

Zhenka was the freest person in the whole world. Maybe also free of any sexual orientation. She chose science as her partner, and together they poked about, studying now some yeast, now some worms, and of late involving themselves in studies of the human genome in a lab in Zurich. It was some sort of world project, which Zarifa made fun of, promising Zhenka free legal assistance when she was taken to court for disclosing the Divine Mystery.

The wedding photograph now also hung in their Cyprus house: broad-shouldered Zarifa in a white blazer with a round, brilliantly sparkling bauble on the collar, holding her short-fingered hand on the shoulder of the shyly smiling Musya, both of them standing by the tall window of the restaurant Le Ciel Bleu on the twenty-third floor of the hotel Okura. Zarifa is beaming, Musya is embarrassed. She was unable to utter the word *husband*. And she would not have been able to explain to anyone who, in fact, Zarifa was to her: a protector, a patron, a friend, a lover. A lover lady or a lover man? Of course she knew that only a man could be a husband . . . But she had never met anyone equal to Zarifa either among men or among women, and out of the feeling of admiration and gratitude emerged her love, the admiring love that occurs in student girls for their old professors, in schoolgirls for their female teachers, in boys for their favorite football players.

They were the first couple of this kind from Russia to register their marriage in Amsterdam. In Armenia or Azerbaijan people did not have the foggiest notion of such exotic things . . .

And the wedding, the wedding! It was unforgettable! No matter how Musya begged her not to organize anything, not to invite anyone to this triumph of love, formerly illegal but a year ago legalized by Dutch law, Zarifa invited her Azerbaijani relatives to the wedding, bought them plane tickets and reserved six rooms in the hotel Okura. On her Armenian side Musya invited only her nephew Ashotik, who for a third year had been studying at Zarifa's expense in a business school in London. She decided not to traumatize the rest of the relatives, her parents and her sister. Her father had epileptic fits from time to time; God forbid he should get emotional and crash down right at the wedding . . .

Zarifa's miscalculation and failure were total: the invited Azerbaijani relatives, led by her older brother Saïd, arrived in almost full muster, except for the Karabakh aunt, the sister of her late father the rugmaker, who was unable to overcome her fear of flying. They arrived on the eve of the wedding, and in the evening of the same day, having met the supposed bridegroom, who turned out to be the bride, with one accord left for the airport without saying good-bye, having thereby refused to participate in the forthcoming blasphemy.

"You were right, Musya," snorted Zarifa, when the secretary informed her that the relatives had departed in full muster for Schiphol Airport. "I thought better of them . . . Saïd adored me in my childhood; he's fifteen years older, he was like a father to me. Better than a father . . . Devil take them!"

She shrugged and went to a nearby bar with a reputation for being as gay as could be and invited all those present to her wedding. The table laid for forty persons was filled by several Amsterdam friends and totally unknown people from the bar, gays, transvestites, and beings of indeterminate sex, more likely male than female. They were beautiful to look at, and delightfully arrayed in almost theatrical outfits with fluffy feathers and clinking pieces of metal . . . Their photographs were also present, not on the wall of the

Cyprus house but in the album shown to all those interested in the combined biography of Musya and Zarifa.

During Zarifa's illness Musya lost much weight and now resembled more than ever a long-necked jug with a rounded bottom. She could not eat at all. That evening she peeked into the refrigerator; it was full of food, but Musya only felt the whiff of inedible cold. She took a shower and went to bed. She sank into sleep at once, without any thoughts and presentiments; they had all died in her; only Zarifa's daily orders remained, which she diligently carried out.

She was awakened by the ringing of the telephone. Her heart began to pound—such early calls did not bode anything good. She grabbed the receiver. "Halloo!" it said. She recognized Saïd's voice at once. He said that he was already in Moscow and would take an 8:20 plane and be in Larnaca three hours later. They should meet him . . . Yes, yes, of course, we'll meet you . . .

She called Katya in the hospital. Katya said that Zarifa had been taken to the operating room to change the catheter, and that she had ordered the secretary to go to the bank in the morning.

"Whattodowhattodowhattodo . . ." Musya whispered with dry lips. She had long lost the habit of making decisions, even in choosing a dress. The task that she now faced was formidable, eclipsing all her woes: she is supposed to meet Saïd, who hates her, she has to go to the airport, and what is she going to say to him, and what is he going to say? . . . and what is she going to wear? . . . Zarifa is in the operating room, there is no one to ask . . . He's already flying here . . .

he's in the air, arriving . . . these Azerbaijani men . . . they're even worse than the Armenians . . . She had met Saïd once in her life, when he came to Amsterdam before the wedding, looked at her with fierce eyes, rose, and led away all Zarifa's relatives . . . terrible . . .

"Tell Zarifa I'm already in the car. Going to meet Saïd . . ."

Musya recognized him at once—he was gray haired, broad, short, but, even so, handsome. The tip of his nose bent slightly down, and the chin, like Zarifa's, bent slightly up and had the same dimple in the middle. In a black two-piece suit and sandals, he looked so absurd that the Greeks followed him with their eyes. On top of that he was hung all over with parcels and was pulling a bag on wheels, of a tropical color, with an enormous package sticking out of it. Seeing him, Musya almost wept, he looked so much like Zarifa. In truth, by his looks he could be her father.

Musya went up to him.

"Good morning, Saïd, I've come to meet you. Zarifa sent me."

"Why didn't she come herself?"

Musya gave him her meek smile.

"She's not feeling well. She's in the hospital. We'll stop to see her first, and then I'll put you up as you prefer—at home or in a hotel . . . You wait here, I left the car in the parking lot . . . I'll pick you up in five minutes."

The BMW was a big car, but the trunk was not so big. They put in his packages. He folded the bag on wheels. Stuffed the huge package sewn up in dirty canvas into the trunk. They drove silently for quite a while, then Saïd asked:

"What's her illness?"

"Cancer," Musya answered curtly.

"Bad. Ours all die of cancer. Father died of cancer, Father's father of cancer. And his father—the stomach. Probably it was also cancer, but they didn't know."

Two hours later Saïd entered the ward where they had just brought Zarifa from the operating room. Naturally swarthy, her yellowed face had now acquired a walnut tint. She opened her eyes, saw her brother. His eyes were filled with horror.

"Ah, you've come . . . Everybody leave, I need to speak to him . . ."

Musya, Katya, and the nurse stepped out one after another, closed the door. Musya stood by the door trying to listen to what the talk was about, but heard nothing—they spoke softly.

Afterward Musya drove the petrified Saïd to the hotel. He declined to go to their house, and she sighed with relief.

The next day, toward evening, Zhenya Raikhman landed at Larnaca Airport. She rented a car and drove to their house. She had been there more than once. The housekeeper Katya met her, called Musya in the hospital; Musya asked Zarifa whether Zhenya should come to the hospital at once. Zarifa told her to come immediately. Zhenya went.

Again Zarifa told everyone to step out. When they were alone, she said to Zhenya:

"It's good that you came, I have three important questions to ask you."

Zhenya, who from the first moment had appraised the situation, did not joke her way out of it in her usual clownish way. She sat down by Zarifa's bed and asked her an inappropriate and even stupid question: "How do you feel?"

"Can't you see for yourself? I'm croaking. It's the fucking

end. And in view of that, I have some questions for you. You are our most intelligent friend . . ."

Zhenya was terrified—not because Zarifa was dying, and not because she was aware of it. They used to live in the same house, in the same apartment in Maryina Grove, when Zarifa was renting a room from Zhenya's aunt, her first place in Moscow, and they knew each other very well. "She'll talk about money, about property," Zhenya thought in fear. Some complicated carving up, a scheme, an intrigue, for which Zarifa was so talented and which evoked in Zhenya an enduring revulsion.

"Not for anything," Zhenya decided to herself. "I'll tell her she should write a will, that's what I'll tell her . . ." And she nervously awaited the question.

Zarifa raised her head slightly.

"Zhenka, tell me, what do you think the intelligentsia is?"

Zhenya inhaled the cool air-conditioned air and exhaled it. Lost her mind? Or is there something I don't understand?

"The intelligentsia?" Zhenya repeated, not believing her ears, but somewhat relieved.

Zarifa closed her eyes and one could see how deeply they were sunk. The black makeup of death had already painted her eyelids, her plump lips had darkened and shrunk, her temples also sank . . . one could see that she was tired, very tired. When she closed her eyes and fell silent, it looked as if she was dead.

"You know, I'm not sure the intelligentsia still exists at all. But if it does, its most precise definition, I think, would be as a strata of educated people whose activity is motivated by general good, not by self-interest . . ."

A shadow of displeasure passed over Zarifa's face.

"No, I don't think so."

Then she opened her eyes and asked as teachers ask at examinations:

"Tell me, what's the difference between Armenians and Azerbaijanis? Not as in backyard disputes. Scientifically. You're a geneticist, after all."

At this point Zhenya, an atheist, blank as a wall in regard to any religious constructions, prayed for the first time in her life: "Help me, Lord! Help me, I can't . . ."

"Are you serious?"

"Yes, I am. I've long wanted to ask you, but I had no time . . ."

"Listen, then. I'll give you a brief lecture . . . It's now considered proven that cognitive and mental characteristics are genetically programmed. But personal particularities constitute a rather broad spectrum and are determined by genetic variants. The frequency of the specific variants in the gene pool of a population . . ."

"Simpler," Zarifa asked, very softly.

"I'll try. In any given population, the most frequent behavioral alleles, that is, variants of the same gene, determine something that is called national character."

"Still simpler, please. It's important for me to understand . . ."

Zhenya paused and again prayed to heaven with all the intensity of someone driven into a dead end.

"All right, here's an example: comparatively recently scientists discovered the existence of the genes that determine bellicosity or peaceful disposition. It's generally thought that the most peaceful people are the bushmen of the Kung-San tribe in southern Africa. The most bellicose are the Yanomamo Indians of South America. It turned out that the Indians possess a 7R mutation of one gene, which makes them bellicose and aggressive in comparison to the bushmen . . ."

"Zhenka, tell me about Armenians and Azerbaijanis . . . I have no need of Indians."

The stream of coolness from the air conditioner blew right on Zhenya's neck, but she felt hot all over.

"You see, besides the purely genetic factors, there are also ethnographic, historical ones, but it is precisely the frequency of the behavioral alleles in a population that characterizes what is conventionally called a national character or ethnopsychological particularities . . ."

"Phooey on you," Zarifa cursed, and her voice sounded quite energetic. "Explain to me why it's impossible to seat Armenians and Azerbaijanis at the same table."

"I suppose this isn't a question of genetics, but a sociocultural one . . ."

"Again you can't give me a sensible answer. Sit down, Zero. Then tell me honestly: am I a good person?"

Zhenya pondered for a moment: she loved Zarifa, but she knew that Zarifa was a multifaceted person, sometimes a good one, even very good, and sometimes . . . oh-ho-ho . . .

Zarifa lay there, broad, flat, with her eyes closed, waiting for an answer.

"You are a very good person . . ." Zhenya said softly and thought, "So many people in the world wouldn't agree with that . . ."

"All right, go." Zarifa opened her eyes and caught Zhenka's gaze with an effort. "Thank you for having come," she said in a displeased and indistinct voice.

Zhenya went out into the corridor, waved her hand, and Musya, Katya, and the hired nurse filed in on tiptoe. The nurse looked at the monitor that hung on the wall, touched Zarifa's hand. The hand lay limp and unresponsive. Zarifa was totally tuned out.

Zhenya was weeping in the corridor.

That night Zarifa died. Musya stayed with her to the last moment. The doctor, who looked at the monitor more often than at the departing patient, was also there. The infrequently quivering line on the monitor leveled out, and Zarifa was no more.

Musya did not weep. She stayed by Zarifa till morning, telling her something she had not managed to tell her in the seventeen years of their life together. In the morning they brought Musya home. As soon as they entered the house, a phone call came from the Armenian sorceress who was supposed to secure the substitution. The sorceress had found out about Zarifa's death from her supernatural channels of communication.

"Listen to me, Anaïd," said the sorceress Margarita, the only one who called Musya by her former name. "They didn't allow us to do what you asked. They don't change the protocol. Call me in a week, I'll tell you something important. Not now. They said she should be buried as a Christian . . ."

"How is it, Margot—as a Christian? She wasn't baptized. They're Muslims . . ."

"I don't know. That's what I was told. I'm just informing you. That a memorial service should be celebrated . . ."

For further actions Musya had instructions in an envelope, inscribed in Zarifa's big handwriting: "To open after my death." Musya opened it, read the instructions, and began to carry them out. She took out of the wardrobe the hanger on which Zarifa, before going to the hospital, had put the outfit for her funeral. It was custom-made by a fashionable dressmaker in Milan during her last trip to Italy. It was white with dense golden embroidery on the collar and cuffs, with a matching golden scarf, and golden mules. It was all new, never worn, as was proper. In a separate bag on the same hanger was white linen underwear.

It was written further about some rug which, if her brother brought it, should be put on the coffin at the leave-taking. And that the leave-taking should be organized in their house in the drawing room. And which restaurant to go to after the funeral. And that there should be a cremation, and, once they got the urn, they should scatter the ashes over the sea. And also about the will, in which everything was described and prescribed, and where to find it.

Musya's only perplexity was the sorceress's instruction about the Christian memorial service. There was no one to ask now. She mentally asked Zarifa, but her question went unanswered.

"She doesn't want it," Musya understood.

The next morning at dawn the coffin was brought to the house.

Musya, who had not slept for three nights, sat down in an armchair by the closed coffin in the drawing room and tuned out.

The leave-taking was appointed for ten o'clock. Zhenya spent the morning putting flowers everywhere, walking around the house like a shadow . . .

At eight o'clock Ashotik, Musya's nephew, arrived from London. He was a slight, oriental man with great mathematical abilities and not-so-great pushiness. Zarifa had helped him on from an early age and by now he had become a slightly slow but reliable top manager. Musya hugged her nephew.

"Thank you for coming, Ashotik."

"What else? I owe her everything."

"Our decent boy," Musya thought. She was still unable to weep.

At nine Saïd arrived from the hotel with a huge package. They ripped off the covering and spread on the floor the Karabakh rug woven by their great-grandfather or maybe his father—in the old days all the men in their family in Shusha were rugmakers. They took the rather heavy rug by four corners, lifted it up, and carefully covered the coffin with it. Now Musya saw the Dragon Zarifa had mentioned to Saïd on the phone.

It was not alone, this Dragon; it was locked in deadly and endless combat with a Phoenix. Sharp corners and angles of ornaments were fighting along the red-and-blue edges, and in the center one could make out a skinny Dragon tied into a ring with a sacred bird. A Phoenix or a Simurgh. This ring was as if a memory frozen forever in a combat from which no one could emerge victorious. The sharp points of claws and teeth were woven by the hands of the rugmaker for all eternity, until the colors faded, until the wool decomposed, until time ground into dust the memory of an artist's work, of the opposing forces of nature and myth, of the enmity of weak people—the memory that lives so deeply in the consciousness of two neighboring peoples, one of which is a monstrous dragon, the other a sacred bird, or the other way round: one is a sacred dragon, the other a monstrous bird . . . and the memory is much deeper than in this handmade picture. It is impossible to tell who in it is the warrior, who the sorcerer, who is evil and who is good, because they are bound forever into one immobile and indissoluble ring . . .

People were arriving. Zhenya took them to the drawing

room: Zarifa's acquaintances, neighbors, even two clients from London . . .

Musya saw, saw this dragon, rushed to the coffin, spread her arms over the rug, and uttered a loud "A-a-a . . ."

This long and resounding cry finally opened the stream that had been held inside her by an inexplicable dam and now poured out along with hot tears. Whether she sang or wept . . . no one understood the Armenian words she was weeping or singing out . . . no one will comfort me, no one will pity me, my life has left me . . .

This cry had the same ancient force that was depicted, woven by the long-dead Azerbaijani artisan, and they merged into one, and everyone in the room wept.

Sunlight poured through the windows, the sound of breakers rose from the sea, as the farewell of two loving souls was taking place, and Saïd, who came to take leave of his sister, whom he loved and whom he had once cursed, also wept. Who was the husband, who the wife, no one cared . . .

The last cry died away on a high ringing note. Saïd came up to Musya, put his arm around her shoulders: "Don't weep, little girl . . ."

The Dragon and the Phoenix were transfixed in their eternal ring.

A week later Musya received the urn with the ashes and scattered them over the sea. Then she packed a small suitcase—Zarifa's, for business trips, when she flew to European capitals on her legal business—and flew to Shusha, to the sorceress Margot, to find out what the important thing was that the sorceress had told her about. She was so used to being guided . . .

Alisa Buys Death

For Tanya Rakhmanova

By the time life was brought to perfection old age arrived. The last, costly touch was a small bathtub installed after a lot of reflection and searching. Some recommended that she get a stall shower, but Alisa resolutely rejected having a vertical bath with a door: what good is water raining down on your head? It's so much better to lie in warm water with a rubber pillow under your head, your softened feet rolling two pleasantly prickly plastic balls . . .

Alisa belonged to the rare breed of people who know with perfect certainty what they want and what they don't want under any circumstances.

From an early age the mixed blood, half-Baltic, half-Polish, she inherited from her mother had cooled off all Alisa's passionate impulses, and the fear of falling into another person's power was stronger than all other fears proper to women: of solitude, of childlessness, of poverty. Her mother, Martha, who had married an army officer back before the war—from which marriage Alisa was born—buried her general, and for the rest of her still young life was always passionately in love and suffered spectacularly, to the point of the psycho wards. She was always ready to bring to her next lover's feet everything she owned, including the apartment her general had left her.

After breaking up with her latest lover, Martha committed suicide in an indecently literary manner: having gone to the hairdresser and manicurist, she threw herself under a train. In Alisa this insane behavior of her mother totally paralyzed any ability to make a futile and fruitless self-sacrifice.

Several former lovers came to Martha's funeral, including the last one, who had abandoned her, thereby inflicting the deadly blow. They unloaded a mountain of flowers on the closed coffin, and the twenty-year-old Alisa, with her pale, not quite developed loveliness, despising and ashamed of her mother's excessive sensuality, swore to herself that she would never become, like her mother, the plaything of such animals. And she didn't. Hers was not a burdensome asceticism, but one of rare, insignificant affairs that put her on a par with her peers in life experience.

She worked as an engineering draftsman, was pleased with her excellent performance, knew that no one in her office was able to draw a line better than she did. At the end of the twentieth century computers appeared, and all the draftsmen, even the most distinguished, had to put away their pencils and suffer over mastering the program that gave precise commands: "Raise the pen, lower the pen, shift to the point . . ." But at this point Alisa shifted to retirement.

The happiest part of her life lasted more than ten years: her pension was small, but Alisa found an excellent way of adding to it—three times a week, from ten till lunch, she walked with children in a garden. After that she was delightfully free. Occasionally she went to theaters, more often to concerts in the Conservatory, made interesting acquaintances there, and lived for her own good pleasure until one day, out of the blue, she fell down unconscious next to the couch in her own apartment. Having lain there for some time, she came to and was astonished by the strange angle of vision: the broken cup in a shallow puddle, the legs of the overturned chair, the nappy red-and-blue rug right by her face. She got up easily. There was a pain in her elbow. She thought a bit and called the doctor. The doctor took her blood pressure and prescribed some pills. Everything seemed to be the same as before. With one exception: from that day Alisa began to think about death.

She did not have any relatives to speak of. The Polish and Lithuanian ones had long vanished from the picture, having no love for the Soviet power represented by the late general. The general's relatives, for their part, had no love either for Martha or for her daughter Alisa, for reasons no one remembered anymore . . .

Alisa was sixty-four. She was in good health, except for the fainting fit that had unexpectedly reminded her of the finiteness of life. However, the question was, What if she gets sick? Bedridden? Who could she count on?

Alisa was unable to sleep. She spent several sleepless nights and came up with a brilliant solution. It was very simple: once she was overcome by illness and it became unbearable, she could poison herself. Prepare a good poison beforehand, best of all some sleeping pills, so that she could take them and not wake up. Without stupidly showing off, as her mother had in her time. Anna Karenina—really! Simply take the pills, and not wake up. And in this way avoid, as it were, the unpleasantness of death . . .

When this thought occurred to Alisa, she jumped out of bed and opened the drawer, where she knew there was a white porcelain box for powder or some other cosmetics left from her mother. She could put the pills in the box, keep it by the bed, and once the time came—take them.

Not yet, not tomorrow. But now was the time to think. First of all she had to find a reliable doctor, who would give a prescription for the pills in the necessary quantity. Not an easy task, but a feasible one . . .

After the fainting fit, Alisa lived as usual, took Arsiusha and Galochka for walks. They were sweet kids from the same building; their mother, a well-bred woman, not some crude bitch, gave music lessons in the morning, and in the afternoon took care of her children.

Alisa spent evenings going to concerts and theaters as before, but she did not forget about a good doctor. She fell to talking with one of her fellow theatergoers. They talked about this and that, and it turned out that her brother was a doctor. Incidentally a Jew. So there. Maybe there was something in what people said about them—saboteurs, poisoners . . . In short, Alisa asked her acquaintance to bring her together with her brother for a medical consultation.

A week later the brother, Alexander Yefimovich, came. A sad, thin man with a questioning expression on his face. He thought that he had been invited for a private medical visit, but Alisa seated him at the table, served tea. He was a bit perplexed, but the patient was well-bred, with a very attractive appearance. Such women had never before entered his field of vision. Truth be told, it was long since any women had entered his field of vision. His female patients he considered strictly from a medical point of view. For three years he had been a widower, languished in solitude, and refused to listen to the hints of his relatives about the harmfulness of being alone.

The table was laid elegantly, fine china cups were set on a gray linen tablecloth; the candy was imported, small, not like hefty Russian "Bears in the Pine Forest." Alisa Fedorovna herself was like her cups and candy: graceful, with thin unsmiling lips, pale blond hair smoothly pulled back. She poured him tea and told him her problem directly: I need strong sleeping pills, in such quantity that if I take them I will not wake up.

Alexander Yefimovich thought a little, took a sip of tea, and asked:

"Do you suffer from an oncological condition?"

"No, I'm in perfect health. The thing is that I would like to be healthy when I pass away. At the moment when I decide to do it. I have no relatives who could take care of me, and I don't have the slightest wish to linger in hospitals, suffering and urinating in my bed. I need sleeping pills so that I can take them once my decision is made. I simply want to buy myself an easy death. Do you see anything bad in that?"

"How old are you?" The doctor, after a long pause, asked a perfectly medical question.

"Sixty-four."

"You look wonderfully well. No one could give you more than fifty," he observed.

"I know. But I did not invite you to pay me compliments. Tell me definitively whether you could prescribe me the necessary medicine in a sufficient dose . . ."

The doctor took his glasses off, set them down in front of him, and rubbed his eyes.

"I need to think. You see, in principle barbiturates are prescribed in a special way . . . it's a matter of legality."

"But in this case it's very well paid," Alisa Fedorovna said dryly.

"I'm a doctor, and for me it's a moral question, first of all. I confess, it's the first time in my life that I've met with such a request."

They finished the tea. They parted, with the doctor promising to think it over and to call and tell her what he decides.

Now it was Alexander Yefimovich who could not sleep. She would not leave his head, this thin, pallid woman, so unlike any he had met in his life. Most unlike his wife, Raya, cheerful, with constantly straying, crimpled strands of hair, with cardigans always threadbare on her big breasts, noisy, even loud . . . and how painfully Raya had departed, eaten up by sarcoma, with bouts of monstrous pain unrelieved by any morphine.

For a whole week he was unable to come to a decision, thinking every day of calling this astonishing Alisa, and being unable to solve the little moral problem she had posed for him. A direct, honest, most worthy woman! It would have been easy for her to complain of insomnia, ask for some sleeping pills, which he would have prescribed, save up ten or twenty doses—who could check on it?—take them, and fall asleep forever.

Their unplanned meeting occurred in the Conservatory, at Pletnev's concert, in the intermission after the suite from Tchaikovsky's *Sleeping Beauty* and before a Chopin sonata. Alisa did not recognize him at first, but he recognized her— instantly. She stood at the bar with a glass of water, looking around for a free chair. Alexander Yefimovich bowed to her from a distance, rose, nodded in invitation, and she sat down on his vacated chair . . .

After the concert he went to accompany her home. While they were listening to music it had been pouring rain. Spreading puddles covered the whole street, and the bronze Tchaikovsky in his bronze chair sat in a small pool of rainwater. The doctor took Alisa Fedorovna's arm. Her arm was light and firm—as his wife Raya's had been when he first accompanied her after the high school prom. He walked along marveling at this long-forgotten tactile sensation.

"Here's a man who doesn't want anything from me," thought Alisa. "It's I who expect a favor from him."

They talked about Pletnev, he mentioned Yudina, observing that since her death it had been Pletnev who represented the type of musician who takes on the right to a new personal interpretation of musical classics. Alisa Fedorovna realized that she was talking to a man who felt music deeply, like a professional, not as a superficial listener like herself.

He confidently brought her right to her house, finding without any difficulty in the depth of the unlit courtyard the two-story annex he had visited a week earlier. He had an excellent sense of orientation both in the forest and in the city: he easily found a place he had seen once. They stopped at the entrance.

He was already taking his leave, but she could not bring herself to ask the question for which she had invited him a week ago.

There was an awkward pause, which he broke with the same questioning expression that was peculiar to him.

"Alisa Fedorovna, I'm ready to accede to your request, but I would like to come to this question later, when . . ." he was clearly struggling to find the right words, "when the circumstances are ripe. Till then I take upon myself the care of your health."

She nodded. No one had ever taken up the care of her, and she would not have allowed it! But it felt good to hear it. She offered him her light, firm hand and took hold of the door handle. The entryway was dark.

"Allow me . . ." He took a step and followed her into the damp darkness.

In the darkness she was feeling for the first step with her foot and tripped slightly. He caught her from behind.

This was how their love affair started—the falling back into youth from a chance touching, the first kiss in the entryway, the burn of the unexpectedness, the feeling of complete trust in the man in Alisa's soul.

And Alisa entrusted more to him than women entrust when young—not her life, but her death.

The happiest year in Alisa's life began. Alexander Yefimovich did not disturb the soft cocoon of solitude which Alisa had woven and in which she felt herself protected. In an astonishing way he even strengthened this protection. As if he provided her with cover from above. What particularly amazed Alisa was Alexander Yefimovich's ability to guess her whimsical taste. Without asking a single question about what she preferred, he brought her firm green apples and pink marshmallows, her favorite stripy caramel, lilacs not white but purple, and the special Kostromskoy cheese. Everything she liked.

Alisa was always sensitive to smells, and all the men with whom she had once had any relationships had smelled of metal, or tobacco, or some animal, but this lover of her old age smelled of mild baby soap, with which he washed his doctoral hands before and after the examination of each patient. With the very soap Alisa had always preferred to all those strawberry and other artificial scents . . .

Alexander Yefimovich, who had lived all his life next to a powerful and demanding woman with extensive needs, tireless in having various, mutually exclusive desires, discovered for the first time that it was possible next to a woman to be free of inexhaustible female power. Reserved Alisa, timid even in the moments of intimacy, radiated silent gratitude. At the end of his sixth decade he felt himself not a lifelong hired serviceman but a generous giver of joy. In the moments of tenderness they called each other by the same teenage name: Alik.

Alexander Yefimovich had worked for many years as a neurologist in the clinic of the RTS, the Russian Theater Society, and owing to his patients had vast connections. He took Alisa on weekdays to the best performances of the season, to the Conservatory, and on Saturdays came to her place for an intimate supper. For the first time in her life Alisa cooked not for herself alone . . .

Life changed, age retreated, and only one thing was troubling: somewhere far off hovered the nagging thought that this unplanned happiness could not last.

Alisa knew that after his wife's death he had lived with his younger unmarried daughter, Marina, who was not quite healthy and not quite happy. The older Anya, healthy and happy, had long lived separately with her husband and two school-age children.

During the whole winter they met like enamored teenagers, and in the summer they went on vacation together, disrupting the plans of the younger daughter, who was used to spending summer vacations with her parents. But Alexander Yefimovich did not inform Alisa of this upsetting conflict with his daughter. He bought two travel vouchers to Komarovo, and in the middle of the summer, when the white nights dimmed and the cool Petersburg heat was not tiring, they arrived at the House of Creativity.

They stayed in separate rooms at opposite ends of the corridor and were both amused by the mutual evening visits.

"You and I, Alik, are like schoolchildren hiding from parental eyes," laughed Alexander Yefimovich when Alisa opened the door for him after a faint rhythmic knocking.

Alisa only smiled mysteriously in response to the joke: the first and sluggish love affair in her life had occurred five years after her mother's death, when her classmates and peers had already managed to acquire husbands, children, and lovers, to get divorced and marry again, and so she had no idea of precisely how teenagers conceal their love affairs from their parents. Her mother Martha never thought of concealing her affairs from Alisa; they were all well displayed, and Alisa had suffered from their noisy passions.

All that Alisa had lacked in her youth was showered on her in her old age, and she was slightly embarrassed by her status as a mistress, especially in the mornings, when they went down to the restaurant filled almost uniformly with elderly couples long weary of their marriages. After breakfast they went on lengthy promenades, occasionally missing lunch and returning only toward evening. This was their first time in the Finnish land; they knew little about its history and geography, and wandered at random, now crossing the dunes and coming out to the sandy beach with its occasional boulders forgotten on the shore in the Ice Age, now straying to Pike Lake, where bathing was much more pleasant than in the Finnish bay overgrown with some brownish slime.

At the lake they met Alexander Yefimovich's acquaintance, an actor and former patient, who had lived in Leningrad and was an old-timer in these parts. He sat with his sleepy fishing rod in the fruitless hope of catching if not a pike then at least a small perch, and was glad to see the doctor. On learning that the doctor and Alisa were in these parts for the first time, he volunteered to show them the former Kellomäki. He took them around the village, showing them the old Finnish dachas, those that had not been dismantled and taken to Finland when this land became Russian, brought them to Shostakovich's dacha, to Akhmatova's cabin, restored and painted a cheerful green, to the dachas of the very-little-known academician Komarov and the very-well-known academician Pavlov . . . For three days they walked around with this volunteer guide, then broke away from him and wandered in a sparse forest gathering blueberries and sour raspberries . . .

The twenty-four days of the voucher went on endlessly, and in the course of those long days and short nights they became as close as if behind them were many years of living together.

When they returned to Moscow, Alexander Yefimovich proposed. Alisa was silent for a long time and then reminded him of her request, with which he had never complied. He had managed to forget what it was about. The sleeping pills . . .

"Alisa, Alinka, why? Why on earth now?"

"Especially now," smiled Alisa.

"I don't understand . . ."

"Because this is going to end . . . and I want to be prepared."

He already knew that it was useless to argue with Alisa.

"This is madness. But I accept."

Alisa took the little porcelain box out of the drawer and handed it to Alexander Yefimovich.

"Put them in here."

This was some shift of consciousness, but there was nothing he could do about it.

"All right, all right. But first we'll get married. And then I'll put them in here—as a wedding present."

He laughed, but he received no smile in response.

"This marriage . . . Isn't it ridiculous? And what will your daughters say?"

"That doesn't matter in the least," he said, and fell to thinking. For the younger, the unsettled one, with her unstable psychology, it could be a real blow . . .

In the fall, soon after the first anniversary of their acquaintance, Alexander Yefimovich turned seventy. He organized a modest tea party at work and received as a gift from his colleagues a new leather briefcase, which differed from the old one only in the number on the silver badge—70 instead of 60.

For friends and family he organized a dinner at the Anchor restaurant. Alisa did not want to come. He insisted—this would be the best occasion to meet his daughters. Alexander kept advancing, Alisa kept retreating. He had already introduced her earlier to his close friends, his schoolmates Kostia and Aliona, and his fellow students the psychiatrist Tobolsky and the obstetrician Pritsker. His family was the last hurdle.

After some hesitation, he invited his brother, who had introduced them, and Musya Turman, his late wife's closest friend. This was a risky gesture, but strategically faultless. He was conducting his preparations on a broad front.

Alisa still hung back. She fussed till the last moment, now consenting to go to this reception, then refusing. She had long grown accustomed to being a queen: it was of no importance to her whether she was liked by those around her or not—queens do not feel this dependence on other people's opinions . . . But here she became anxious and immediately felt annoyed with herself.

Alexander Yefimovich managed to persuade her an hour before leaving home: "You mean too much to me, I can no longer conceal you. Besides I have to prepare them all . . ."

And she surrendered.

They came almost simultaneously; by ten past seven the guests were all sitting at the table.

"I would like you to meet Alisa Fedorovna," Alexander Yefimovich proudly announced and introduced each guest in turn to Alisa: Anya with her husband and the two grandchildren, Marina, Musya Turman. His friends had already had occasion to meet her before.

Alisa was impeccable and she knew it. Her silk top of tobacco color was caught at the slender waist with a soft leather belt, and hers was the only waist among the barrel-like figures of the other ladies. The guests were somewhat stunned, even the daughters, who had been warned that their father had invited his lady friend. Musya Turman sat there speechless—she glanced at this person with the late Raya's eyes and felt insulted.

"Nothing to look at," she whispered to Anya. But Anya did not second her.

"Why, Aunt Musya, she's a very interesting woman. And her figure . . ."

"Figure, figure!" Musya snorted. "She's a manipulator. She'll show herself, just mark my words!"

But the waiter was already pouring champagne, and the friend Kostya raised his glass.

Kostya, gray-haired, jowly, rotund, began to speak: Sashka and he had known each other for sixty-seven years out of seventy, knew each other so well that sometimes they couldn't tell where the boundary between their thoughts was, that he no longer knew who first said, who first thought, that they were more than friends and more than brothers, and that all his life he, Kostya, had followed after and never caught up with him . . . and there were more words, all of them praiseful and somehow merry. And in the end he said that he was glad to see next to Sashka the magical Alisa, who came to us from Wonderland. Alisa produced a cool smile . . .

A month later they quietly and casually registered their marriage. Alexander Yefimovich fulfilled his promise: the little porcelain box, filled with little white pills, sat on the desk next to a stack of writing paper, envelopes, and outdated subway tickets.

With astonishing delicacy Alexander Yefimovich introduced himself into Alisa's apartment, without disrupting anything in it, but, on the contrary, solidly repairing everything that hung on a string or had been held together with scotch tape. He fixed the loose branch of a chandelier, replaced the burner that had long been out of order, and Alisa had an ever-strengthening feeling that his medical profession extended to curing everything he touched. Without any extraneous help the plant on the windowsill began to bloom—something it had never done before.

The spouses, who had had no complaints about their health even before, grew visibly younger.

"The hormonal cycles have started over," the husband laughed.

Toward spring another unforeseen and improbable event came to light: Alexander Yefimovich's almost forty-year-old younger daughter Marina was pregnant. Her birth defect—a hare lip and cleft palate—and the small scars left on her face by a quite successful surgery, had distorted her character more than her appearance. Since childhood she had been avoiding all company and had chosen the career of a proofreader, which allowed her to keep company only with texts and not with people. Her father was amazed by the fact of her pregnancy. However, he was rather glad, understanding that he would not leave his daughter alone but with a child who could replace for her the whole world, which she regarded as hostile.

Alisa nodded vaguely: she had her own reasoning concerning childbearing, but she felt no need to share it with her husband. The less so as her reasoning had long since lost all topical interest.

When Alexander Yefimovich shared his news with Alisa, the pregnancy had been concealed in the fat stomach for six months already, but was imperceptible even to an attentive eye. Marina was the same fat, flabby woman she had been since her youth.

When the time of the delivery drew near, the father arranged for his daughter, old for a first childbearing, to enter a good maternity hospital on Shabolovka Street, where his former fellow student Pritsker was the head of the department. Given Marina's age and weight, it was decided to perform a cesarean section. The surgery was scheduled for Tuesday morning. Alexander Yefimovich waited for the call from the surgeon and was informed that all was well—the baby girl was without any defects, at least without a hare lip. Alexander Yefimovich still remembered the horror he had experienced when his wife came out of the hospital with a little girl with a yawning triangular hole from mouth to nose. Now he sighed with relief.

"So I'll go to the hospital," he said to Alisa.

They put together a package of food for the new mother: kefir, milk, candies, and a piece of cheese. He left the house and had a stroke of luck: he saw that beautiful, fresh hyacinths—Alisa's favorite—had just been delivered to the nearby florist, and he bought a big bouquet for his daughter and for the nurses. The salesgirl wrapped the bouquet in gift paper. He went out to the deserted street in the calm after lunchtime with the flowers and the plastic bag of food. There was a thinnish crowd waiting for the bus. He kept a little away to protect the beautiful hyacinths from the jostling people when the bus arrived.

Just then a big black car, driving at high speed in the middle of the street, collided with another as big and black, and was thrown over to the sidewalk. It ran into a lamppost, knocking down three people on its way. One, with a bouquet of flowers, was killed . . .

In the evening Alisa called Pritsker. He said that everything was fine with Marina and the baby, but that Alexander had not come. Alisa began to make phone calls. Fifteen minutes later she was told that her husband was in the morgue. They had spent the whole day trying to find the family, but at his home address no one answered the phone.

That was the end. "Yes, yes, I've been expecting something like that." The porcelain box in the drawer . . .

Alisa began the next morning with the hospital—took the milk, kefir, and cheese to Marina. Then she went to the morgue. The funeral was delayed because of the forensic examination.

Marina was told about her father's death only three days later. She had a mental breakdown, and Alexander Yefimovich's other friend, Professor Tobolsky, took her to Kashchenko Institute. For the time being the girl stayed in the hospital . . . Anya, Marina's older sister, was unable to take the baby—her husband, who could not stand Marina, rebelled.

Two weeks later the baby was taken from the maternity hospital by her grandmother, Alisa Fedorovna. Alisa had had a premonition that her happiness with Alexander Yefimovich would not last, but the premonition had told her nothing about the newborn baby.

The girl lived in a pram next to Alisa's bed. Alisa did not want to move to her husband's bigger apartment. There everything was dirty, and the bathtub with its cracked enamel was awful, and here there was a new one, shiningly white.

Marina was discharged from the psychiatric hospital only after six months. But how could little Alexandra be entrusted to this flabby, slovenly, psychologically troubled woman?

The box with the barbiturates was still in the drawer, but Alisa could no longer make use of her husband's wedding present. That is, theoretically she could. Sometime . . . when the circumstances were ripe . . .

A Foreigner

A woman, her body flattened on the sides and with resolute breasts, was studying out of the corner of her eye a young man sitting at the other end of a garden bench buried in a newspaper. There was something she liked about him. Maybe it was the newspaper. She liked men who read newspapers. Her first, short-lived husband, an engineer killed by an explosion in a factory workshop, used to go out before breakfast on Sundays to buy a newspaper. And the second, the present one, also read newspapers in the morning. He brought them from work, in fact, and they were always yesterday's. This one, on the bench, was also reading a newspaper.

"A foreign one!" Her sidelong glance caught the big wavy letters of the title. "Why not! It's even more interesting!"

She moved closer and poked her finger at the newspaper: "What's this language?"

The man with the newspaper was a bit startled and turned his whole body toward her.

"What did you ask?"

"A real foreigner!" the woman thought happily.

"I mean, these are interesting letters, what's this language you're reading?"

"It's Arabic," the young man answered amiably. And

thought, "Must be a prostitute." The dyed blonde, over forty, moved still closer to him. The handbag with its metal clasp that she pressed to her considerable stomach dispersed his doubt: Definitely a prostitute . . .

He was twenty-seven. It was the second year of his life in Moscow. And not just anywhere, but at the graduate students' dormitory of Moscow University, in the L building. He had long decided to find a woman for himself—all his dormitory neighbors brought in some women, with a pass or on the sly past the supervisor and the floor attendants. And no one minded. Only he still could not bring himself to do it.

"Such pretty letters, even better than ours!" the woman said with a false smile, but he did not understand what she said. He was a mathematician, a graduate student of a famous professor, with whom he talked in English, and what are mathematicians' talks, really? Their understanding is without words, on a higher level of symbols incomprehensible to simple mortals. Of course he studied Russian, but had not made much progress . . . The wrinkles on his brow betrayed the working of his thought—he kept trying to construct a simple phrase: "What was the cost of her services?" This was the occasion he had long been waiting for, and now he suddenly lost courage, became embarrassed, afraid that nothing would come of it . . . He had never ever dealt with a woman. Never even held a girl's hand. At home in his village, as soon as they grew up they were wrapped in impenetrable dresses and shawls, only their eyes showed through the openings, and it was impossible to see anything else. The only women he had ever touched were his mother, his grandmother, his aunts. They were all old. He did not even have any sisters. Only two brothers.

When he was sent to his uncle in Baghdad, to study in

a good school, the rules in the big city were the same. Besides, his choice was—mathematics. This meant one of two things—to get married or to study. On this account Salikh had no doubt: it was to study . . .

"Fancy that, Arabic! My daughter studies English. It's also a difficult language," observed the woman, still peeking at the newspaper from the corner of her eye.

"Your daughter?" he repeated in perplexity.

"Yes, I have a daughter, Lilya, she studies English. An A student!"

"That's good," said the young man and buried himself in the newspaper.

A strange woman! If she is a prostitute, why is she telling me about her daughter? He had already made up his mind to run for it, but the woman raised her arm, put it on the back of the garden bench, and he caught a whiff of such female intimacy that he no longer had any doubts: it will work out, it will. He became nervous, began mentally putting together the phrase that refused to be constructed, and said only: "A-ah . . . a daughter . . . at home?"

The woman laughed: "At home, my daughter is at home. She'll be eighteen soon. A beautiful girl. And you, excuse my asking, are you married?"

He shook his head. The conversation was taking an unexpected direction. He turned toward the woman. She now looked at him more attentively and noticed that he was slightly cross-eyed and generally not all that handsome. But he wore a nice two-piece suit and a tie, and his shoes were clean. An engaging man, he'd do . . .

"What's your name?" The woman resolutely made her move, and he was glad that she took the lead in the game.

"Salikh."

She offered him her hand—a strong, rough hand—and gave his limp one an energetic shake.

"I'm Vera Ivanna. So you're not married? And what are you doing here in Moscow?"

"I'm writing my thesis."

"Ohh!" the woman was glad. "A scientist?"

"A mathematician," he nodded, sinking into total perplexity. The sweet smell of her armpits still hovered around her like smoke around a kebab . . .

"Would you like to get married?"

And everything cleared up—a matchmaker! The woman is a matchmaker! Not a prostitute!

"I would!" he smiled. "I'd like to get married."

Lilka was not like other girls. She had no thoughts of marriage; on the contrary, she despised marriage, because she knew it perfectly well from hearing the morning creaking of the bed, her stepfather Kolya's puffing, and her mother's slight giggling—all of it crowned by the scraping of the basin that was kept under the bed and the sound of pouring water. She woke up to this music at six o'clock, and when she got up at seven no one was there: her mother and Kolya had gone off to work.

Lilya did not keep company with the girls in her building, who began these creaking amusements at an early age, and for that they called her "the stuck-up." And they were right: in fact Lilya was stuck up about her own life, not in a very definite or detailed way, but she knew for certain that she would have a good, well-paying job as an accountant or a teacher; she would have a professional diploma and her own room, a whole room, without a partition; and she would dress not in rustic fashion, like all the women in the building, but in a nice outfit, like a schoolteacher. She would have high-heeled shoes. White . . . Why white? Wasn't it stupid to trudge through the mud in white shoes? But her dream did not consider that. The shoes were white!

Lilka's immediate plans included getting a high school diploma and continuing her education. She had not yet decided where. The nearest to home was the School of Chemistry, but she did not like chemistry. The subject she liked was called English Language, and she found out where she could study it. There were three places: a foreign language school, a teachers college, and the university. Now, at the end of her high school studies, she hesitated whether to go and study English or, after all, to choose accounting courses. In her inexperience she thought that accounting was a moneymaking profession. In short, marriage was not included among the life tasks of her five-year plan. This plan was clear and strict: studies and then, after graduation, marriage by the age of twenty-three, a child by twenty-four, and so on . . . At the moment she had to pass her final exams and was grinding away at her math.

Just then Vera Ivanna came in. Her face bore a mysterious expression. She often assumed it. She would bring a package from work, wave it in the air with this mysterious expression: "What is it I've brought?" That was clear: it would be either some red caviar in wax paper, or a piece of melting butter. A mystery, really. She worked in a hospital kitchen, had access to food, and always filched something from it. This time the expression was there, but there was no package.

"Well, Lilka, you'll never guess what I found for you!" her mother said, arms akimbo. Lilya barely turned her head.

She was preparing for the finals and could not care less for her mother's silly things. But her mother would not stop.

"Lil, Lil, just listen!"

"I have a math test tomorrow, Mom, leave me alone!"

"Maybe I'm about to give you such a present that you'll be thankful for the rest of your life."

Lilya roused herself.

"So you bought me white shoes, did you?"

"What a fool you are, Lilka!" Vera Ivanna was hurt.

The discussion about the white shoes had been going on already for over a month—to buy or not to buy them. Vera Ivanna thought that the commencement ball was not a great enough occasion for buying white shoes: Lilka wore shoes down quickly on one side, and she was sure to ruin the heels, and the shoes would not survive till the wedding.

Besides, white shoes were only for special occasions, while black ones . . . —this was the discussion they had been having.

"What a fool you are! There's business brewing, there'll be white shoes, and a white dress, and all that!"

Lilya roused herself:

"Mom, are you joking or what?"

"Joking, hah! I've found a fiancé for you! A foreigner! There!" Vera Ivanna laid her cards on the table.

"What's this, Mother? I wouldn't even think of thinking about it! What's the need? Forget it! You'll buy me white shoes just the same, and I don't need any shoes if I have to get married for them!" Lilka said resolutely.

"So you'll be a fool, a real fool!" Vera Ivanna became angry.

"You're a fool yourself," Lilya replied impolitely. That

was their way, without Chinese ceremony, with healthy simplicity.

"Look at this smarty! Just like her papa!"

Lilya did not remember her papa—she was two when he was killed. Vera herself had a vague memory of that husband. Although she frequently told her daughter, "You've taken after your papa!" She said it on various occasions: now as if in praise, when she got high grades or was good at chess, now irritably, when she did not wash the floor or failed to do something else she had been asked to do.

Before the war Vera had had many suitors, but when the war began and all worthwhile boys were sent to the front, she became frightened that there would be no men left and married the first one who came along. He was an engineer at a factory, a bald and bespectacled fellow named Schiltz, ten years older than Vera. The good thing about him was the room. It outweighed both the bald spot and the none-too-manly looks. She had lived with him for three years and no one better came along. A daughter was born. And he died when there was an explosion at the factory . . . Vera went on living in Schiltz's room, with her daughter Lilka and her second husband, Kolka. The only thing Lilya knew about her deceased father was the bristly name she bore, because of which she was teased as "shilly-shally" . . .

"He's a student of mathematics, not a dog's prick! A foreigner! I wouldn't recommend you anyone bad!" Vera Ivanna was hurt. "You yourself will never find another one like that!"

Lilya fell to thinking. White shoes also had some weight . . . Mother never threw words to the wind.

The first meeting of the bride and bridegroom was set for a Sunday, at the entrance to the same Hermitage garden. This was a week after the commencement ball, which was Lilya's firm condition—after the finals! Lilka came hobbling to her first rendezvous with her bridegroom in high-heeled white shoes, which her mother bought ahead of time: everyone thought it was for the commencement ball, but Lilya knew it was for the wedding. Vera Ivanna was a bit nervous, though she had called him twice, and they had arranged everything, and he had confirmed his intentions. Of course she worried about the fish getting off the hook, but the bridegroom came at six on the dot to the same place where they had first met each other.

In the past few days Salikh's mind had wandered away from his work; he slept poorly for two nights; he almost decided not to go to this strange blind date. But waking up, he discovered that the decision had been made as if against his will—and he began to prepare. Spent a long time washing, shaving, choosing his tie. He realized that he was violating all the laws and rules of life, but there was nothing he could do: he was gripped by the excitement of the impending marriage . . . The voice of reason told him that his excitement was premature, that the bride could be completely unsuitable; as for his family, it was clear that they would be violently opposed to his willful marriage to a suspicious Russian woman, breaking with all family traditions, and their reaction would be hostile. He was worried not so much about his father as about his stepmother, the keeper of all the rules of life. She never tired of repeating the word *usul,* "order."

The family had always considered Salikh to be special. Allah had made him not for trade, but for something intellectual. In the second year of school, the village teacher told Salikh's father that the boy would have a path different from other children's, and the father sent him to Baghdad, to his younger brother, who traded in fabrics. There he finished an English school, then the university, and studied in graduate school . . . "Maybe I can finally allow myself to live like a European!" he kept saying to himself. And he went to meet his bride . . . almost like a European.

He was a tall man, his right shoulder higher than the left, his head slightly inclined, as if with attention. Most of all Lilya liked his glasses—we don't make them like that: in a thick brown frame, and the very centers of the lenses slightly aslant. Lilya herself was near-sighted and wore glasses, but her frame was junky. He was wearing a light suit, a white shirt, and a yellow necktie. His shoes were also unusual, of a reddish-brown color, with a leather strip across, decorated by little holes. It was immediately obvious that he was a foreigner, especially from his glasses and shoes . . . Lilya had never seen such men—she could not say she liked him in himself, but he evoked her interested respect.

The bridegroom liked the bride from afar: next to the dyed blonde he had already met indistinctly hovered a small, thin-legged girl with big breasts. Not quite blonde, but not a brunette either. As he came closer he noticed that she was wearing glasses and felt the flush of unexpected tenderness and affinity. Iraqi brides never wore glasses; only old women, who had already fulfilled their female mission, could allow themselves to acknowledge poor vision. It was Lilya's glasses that for him were the sign of her unquestionable truthfulness. Women in Russia were beautiful but aroused suspicion: in every beauty Salikh fancied a danger-ous depravity, if not something worse. This girl was not a beauty, but looked very decent.

The girl gave him her hand first, but without any smile, and he liked that, too: a strict one! Said, My name is Lilya. Beautiful!

Half an hour later they were sitting in a café. He ordered coffee and pastry for everyone. The bride's mother ate one pastry, then another. Lilya excused herself: "People are sur-prised, but I don't like sweets."

Ten minutes later Vera Ivanna looked at her watch, said that she had some urgent business, and left. Salikh found himself alone with his bride and was amazed by it. Aston-ishing people! Just like that, on the first day of their acquain-tance, to leave a girl alone with a man . . . No, it wasn't acci-dental that they won the war! Daring people!

"Do you speak English?" the bridegroom asked, just as a test, at random.

Lilya smiled. "I'm the best in my class!"

And Salikh understood that his fate was sealed.

The first thing the bride asked when they were left alone was whether it was true that he was a mathematician. She asked it in English. He said, yes, a mathematician. Moscow University had a strong program in mathematics, that was why he had come here.

"And I hate mathematics," the bride confessed, but the bridegroom did not quite understand. "I don't like it," the bride clarified. "I have A's in all subjects and C's in math."

"That doesn't matter. When we're married, you won't be occupied with mathematics."

"Of course I won't!" laughed the bride. "What an idea!"

They left the café. Lilya was in a hurry to get back home.

He wanted to hail a cab. The bride stopped him and explained, "Why waste money? It's three stops by trolley, right to my house. It costs just four kopecks!"

This pronouncement of economic strategy dispersed the last matrimonial doubts: the inevitability of destiny was there—breasts, glasses, English language, frugality. And Salikh suggested that he and Lilya make an application to hold a wedding. Lilya laughed. "An application to be married, not to hold a wedding. The wedding will come after that!"

"Of course, yes, after that!" the bridegroom agreed.

A decent, a very decent girl. And he took her under the arm. She did not protest. The sleeve of the pink dress was short, the arm was bare and smooth, and white, very white. For the first time in his life Salikh touched a woman.

Lilya spilled the beans. She could not help herself. First she told Zhenka about her fiancé, a foreigner. Then Lyuska about her fiancé, a mathematician. After that there was no need to tell anybody—they all knew that Lilya was going to get married. Vera Ivanna also learned the news in the courtyard as she was coming home from work. Zhenka ran up to her:

"Aunt Vera! When is Lilka's wedding? Is it true he's a foreigner?"

After that everything started moving incredibly quickly. Vera Ivanna thought it all out strategically. She did not invite the fiancé to their place. Although their room was good, a whole two hundred square feet, still it was in a communal apartment. And they were not particularly rich: it was the third year they had been saving up to buy a cupboard, and without a cupboard it all looked rather poor. There was, however, a rug on the wall. But who knows with these foreigners, they may all be used to having whole apartments to themselves.

The bride and bridegroom went to the movies a couple of times, strolled in the Hermitage garden and in Neskuchny Garden. And then they applied to be married at the only registry office in Moscow where they accepted applications from foreigners who wanted to marry lucky Russian girls. The procedure took three months, longer than in ordinary registries . . .

Life had big changes in store for Lilya, but she did not change her general plan. She applied to study in the teachers college, passed the exams, and was accepted. Her mother just waved her hand when she heard about it: "Do as you like, you're your own mistress, and it's for you to account for it to your husband."

"I don't understand you, Mom. Either I'm my own mistress, or I account for it, right? You go and give an account to your Kolya, I won't do any accounting to my husband . . ."

And she did not inform her future husband that she was now a student.

After August, bleak as premature old age, came a honeyed Indian summer, deceptively heralding a blissful break in the routine change of seasons. These last precious days of peacefulness, when nature is free of the duty of fruit bearing, were ideal for marital festivities that promise new germination and new fruit . . . People of the neighborhood usually celebrated weddings in the courtyard of the green lane, which was unfairly called the Church blind alley, although it had ceased to be a blind alley long ago. In place of the two wooden houses that had turned to dust, a street leading to the Burdenko Institute was paved. On the edge of the street, in a little dirt area separated from the rest of the world by a red-brick wall on one side and on the other hidden by three old linden trees, people usually organized funerals and weddings. Two barracks enclosed this scenic area. On ordinary days the dwellers in these barracks engaged in slight hostilities, but for celebrations, holidays, and memorials they united and knocked together a long table for a common cause: to put a coffin on or to hold a wedding feast.

Once the marriage application was made, Vera Ivanna immediately began to reflect on how to better organize everything, so that it would be no worse than other weddings. But also no better . . . But Lilka announced from the first, "No, Mom, I don't want any yokel wedding: we'll go to a restaurant."

Vera Ivanna almost burst with indignation: "You just think how much it will cost to wine and dine the whole crew in a restaurant!"

"Now listen, Mother, to what I tell you. We'll have the wedding at a restaurant, and Salikh and I will invite the guests: you and Kolya, and Aunt Raiska, devil take her. She doesn't know how to behave, but I'll pump her up a bit. Or you talk to her, she's your sister, after all. She should come alone, without that boyfriend of hers. And maybe the two witnesses, Lyuska from my side, and from Salikh's his friend from the embassy. That's all!"

Vera Ivanna raised hell. First she grabbed the laundry line which she had used to "teach" little Lilya what's what. But Lilya showed great firmness and even a certain wisdom:

"Put that rope down! You wanted to get me married, and I'm about to get married. But the rest will be the way I want it. There'll be no yokel marriage. My husband is a foreigner, I'm not going to disgrace myself before him. He'll think we're a bunch of country hicks. I want it to be civilized."

"And your godmother? And your sister-in-law? And Roza Petrovna Yarovaya? And Gena Ziugoshin? There're some forty persons in the barracks, plus relatives. What will people say? We can't do that, Lilya, we can't!"

"I don't want it the way they do it, Mom. They get drunk as fish, they fight, swear at each other. I don't want that."

"She's just like her father! Just like her father!" And, seeing deadly resolution on Lilka's face, Vera Ivanna burst into tears. "How are you going to look people in the eye?"

"I won't! I won't look them in the eye! We'll leave after the wedding, there'll be a sort of a wedding trip, so there . . ."

"Yes, just like her father! Nothing's the same as people do it!" snorted Vera Ivanna, but it was clear to her that the battle was lost.

And that was how it went. The registration in the office was in the morning, in the third week of September. Lilya put on her white shoes, which were still new—she had worn them only three times since the commencement ball. The dress was made of heavy white nylon—Vera Ivanna had obtained it at a mysterious outlet in Podolsk, where simple mortals were not admitted, only government people.

There was a wedding photo: Lilya in a white dress tightly fitted to her abundant breasts—the dressmaker had suffered over it, had to take in six tucks, and the bodice felt like steel armor. The skirt was wide, a full two lengths of four foot width. The post-festival fashion for full skirts was still lingering. But the skirt was not seen in the photo; the double portrait was to the waist—only the high-necked dress and the long sleeves were visible. The groom was wearing a gray suit and a white necktie.

Salikh ordered twelve copies of the photograph. One lived for a long time in Vera Ivanna's room, and she sometimes put it on the wall, sometimes took it down, depending on the phases of the moon, or, more precisely, on the phases of her relations with her daughter and her political zigzags.

The state of Iraq was even worse than ours—there was no way to figure anything out: whether it was East or West, whether they were friends or enemies—and it was impossible to get anything out of Salikh; besides mathematics he did not want to know anything at all. Lilya's stepfather, Kolya, was interested in politics, he wanted to grasp where we stood . . . There was no clarity.

Salikh sent the wedding pictures to his numerous relatives in Iraq by diplomatic mail, provoking utter dismay: he had married God knows who and without following any rules. Fatma-Hanum, Salikh's stepmother, who had received him as an infant from his mother's hands and loved him perhaps more than the two sons she had from Salikh's widowed father, studied this dressed-up photo with mixed feelings of indignation and admiration. She liked this bold girl with cropped hair, and she liked Salikh, who did everything in his life not as custom called for. In the end she wrapped the photograph in a piece of silk and put it in a box.

Of all the numerous people surrounding Salikh in Moscow there were two who merited his attention: the young man Hassan, who worked in the Iraqi Embassy and had a big career looming ahead of him, and the middle-aged Russian mathematician Yakov Khazin, the scientific advisor of Salikh's thesis. The first told him to rent a private apartment for his family life, and the second said that he had never been married and was not going to risk doing it. Salikh followed the first advice without delay: rented a one-room apartment on Leninsky Prospekt, within walking distance of the university, though not very close. Lilya moved in as soon as Salikh got the keys. Thus the first problem the spouses had was resolved: they absolutely refused to live in Schiltz's room, even behind the proposed partitioning curtain, thereby offending the hospitable mother-in-law.

"Good riddance," she snorted, and did not give her daughter any dowry.

Salikh was first surprised, then indignant, and then calmed down. There are different rules everywhere: in fact, he himself did not give any *mahr*—that is, a payment for the bride—nor did he offer the customary three wedding gifts, but only bought two golden rings. And the bride's parents did not organize any wedding: he paid the bill for the dinner in the restaurant, and his in-laws did not even bat an eye.

By the time the engaged couple went to the registry office, Salikh liked his fiancée more and more—particularly her strictness: kissing was out of the question, and her breasts resting in brassiere cups that resembled baby bonnets—something Salikh could not know—alluringly thrust forward, drawing to themselves his whole male being, hastening the time when at last . . . but meanwhile they were untouchable and unattainable.

Resolving the problem took the first three months of the marriage. Lilya's virginity, stubborn and refusing to surrender, distracted him from writing his thesis, because all the powers of his outstanding intellect stalled, and the habitual effort moved to a place little suited to mental creativity.

Right after the wedding, Lilya revealed to her husband something she had previously kept secret: she was now a student, and since the first of September had been attending lectures at the school where she studied to be a teacher. Salikh was surprised: his wife turned out to be an altogether modern woman, she wanted to be educated, and he had respect for this news. His main problem in the first months of the marriage was not his wife's higher education, but her deflowering.

At the end of the third month, after persuasions, tears, resolute actions, serious struggle which—credit must be given to the husband's chivalry—never arrived at outright violence, Salikh reached the desired destination. The bliss consisted in the accomplishment, both well-filled breasts were held, slightly overflowing, in the husband's hands, and the tortured rod broke through the long-resisting obstacle. Both wept—Lilya from the insult and pain, Salikh from a fineness of nervous constitution.

It turned out that the sacred fruit of marriage was set immediately. Lilya was not glad at all: she liked having a foreign husband, but according to her former plan, she was supposed to have a baby after finishing her studies.

The following months passed under the banners of mutual defeat, though neither side noticed it. Lilya was totally ignorant of erotic frolicking. In the backyard of the house she had grown up in, sexual life was considered an interesting indecency, and the foreign word *sex* had not yet entered everyday vocabulary; and she reduced marital rites to a weekly duty. Besides, when it became clear that she was pregnant, she tried to circumvent the duty by referring to natural causes. As for her husband, he was somewhat disappointed: literary descriptions of marital joys were more exciting than their modest reality. On the other hand, he had known since childhood about his intellectual superiority to his brothers and peers: his head was incomparably better than theirs, and he ascribed the ecstasies that were in order for young men in the company of plump women in real life and of virgin houris posthumously to the numerous prejudices of poorly educated people . . .

In all other respects Lilya proved to be an excellent wife: she mastered the skill of the irreproachable ironing of white shirts, of the right way to cook rice, kept the rented apartment immaculately clean, as well as the rug that Salikh had bought as soon as they moved in. Lilya had time for everything and in the mornings went to classes. Salikh liked that in her, too.

Mutual understanding was improving: owing to her studies, Lilya's English was growing more strong and rich. For Salikh this was a pleasant surprise—his Russian was not doing very well. Lilya's spoken English, on the contrary, was lively, and its slight stiffness was quickly improving in her husband's company.

Vera Ivanna, who visited her daughter every once in a while, was at a loss to figure out whether the man she hooked for her daughter was a lucky choice or she had missed the mark. He seemed to be well-to-do, but a bit miserly. Kolya once sidled up to him to borrow some money—some fellow was selling a car from the garage of the Ministry of the Interior, an okay car, not too old, just in need of an overhaul of the motor and it would run for a while. But the son-in-law said right off, "No, I'm a student, my parents still support me. Once I start earning my own money, then we'll talk." Maybe Salikh said it more gently, but Lilya made it sound more emphatic, because she knew how her mother and her dear husband liked to rake everything to their side. Here the newlyweds had full mutual understanding.

Meanwhile Lilya was losing her good looks, spots came out on her moderately beautiful face, her stomach protruded before the usual time—from narrow hips, as the doctor explained. The doctor practiced in a local women's clinic in Degtiarny Lane, near the place of Lilya's official residence. She was an old Jewish woman with a slight mustache and the last name of Berman, and she was more than an acquaintance; all pregnant women of the neighborhood had gone to her since before the war, and Vera Ivanna herself had produced Lilya under her supervision. So this Mrs. Berman grunted each time she examined Lilya, and in the seventh month said it was impossible to avoid a caesarian. That is, it was possible, but it would be better not to risk it, because the first delivery for a woman of such construction posed the danger of failing to give birth . . .

Lilya told none of this to her husband; she allowed him to touch her stomach, or breasts, or whatever else, but not more than that. Her term was coming closer, promising release. At the end of the first year, she successfully passed the exams, in spite of her pregnancy. She decided that next year she would take a leave of absence and look after the baby, and a year later would go back to her studies.

Lilka was placed in the Krupskaya maternity hospital several days before her term, so that the doctors could watch over her and forestall any possible problems. Salikh came under the window only once—visitors were not allowed inside—shouted something incomprehensible, but brought a parcel with apples, kefir, and a letter. The letter said that Salikh's father had died in Sulaymaniyah, and he must urgently go to the funeral.

Lilya gave birth to a baby girl that same evening, exactly a year after the wedding, in the middle of September. Without any caesarian, only out of indignation that her husband had abandoned her on the eve of such an event. The girl bore a ridiculous resemblance to her father, minus the spectacles and mustache.

That was all. The husband vanished. Lilya was brought from the hospital by Vera Ivanna and Kolya. At first Kolya took her in his service car to her rented apartment. There they found the traces of hurried packing, scattered things, and on the table, among the dirty plates and cups, sat a little box which keen-sighted Vera Ivanna was the first to notice. In it was a ring. A diamond ring. The stone was small, but it did glitter. Vera Ivanna quickly grabbed it and put it into her bra, mumbling: "It'll be safer with me."

Lilya kept silent. The baby tactfully kept silent as well. It—that is, she—was used to abundance since birth: milk from her mother's nipples flowed in a continuous stream without any need for effort on the part of the baby's oral apparatus. All the newborns in the maternity ward whose mothers lacked milk were nourished from Lilya's bounties.

Vera Ivanna looked around the hastily abandoned room and told Lilya to come home for the time being and to return to the rented apartment when Salikh came back from the funeral. Lilya, being at a loss, silently accepted.

They went home to Schiltz's apartment. Some moving of furniture was called for—the cupboard had already been bought and now occupied the space where a baby bed could stand. So the Arab girl was put in a basket and given the inappropriate name Victoria. They began to live and wait . . .

For the first few days everyone was silent. Kolya because he was used to being silent, Lilya because she had nothing to say, while Vera Ivanna had a lot to say but tried her best to contain her seething fury against Salikh, who, though a foreigner, had turned out to be a traitor, like all men . . . And against the fool Lilka, who had proved unable to keep her man from leaving. As if the funeral couldn't take place without him!

In reality she was angry with herself. A week later she admitted, I'm an utter fool. It dawned on her that she had been deceived! She thought he was a decent foreigner, but he was an Arab . . . He won't come back. He used Lilya a little—and that was it.

It looked like it was so. Days followed one after another, a month went by, and the husband did not appear . . .

Poor Lilya! She thought that through marriage she had left the backyard and its barracks to ascend to higher spheres, and now her return home, and with the baby besides, meant a terrible downfall.

The rented apartment was paid for till the end of the month. Leaving for the funeral, her husband had not provided either for her or for their baby, and a terrible foreboding came over Lilya: her husband would never come back. As weeks went by, the hope of his return was fading. Especially since there were no letters . . .

It was already the middle of October. By now Lilya felt herself wounded and deceived; she was especially hurt because, like a fool, she had given birth to a child, who now tied her hands. She looked at the girl with perplexity, unable to understand why she had given birth to her. The girl behaved like an angel, as if she understood that her mother had other things to think about. She was very quiet, nursed eagerly, did not wake up too often, and smiled vaguely and prematurely.

At the end of the month the owner of the apartment called and asked them to remove all their belongings. Lilya, her mother, and Kolya drove over to get Salikh's clothing, books, and papers. Initially the two cardboard boxes stayed under the parents' bed; then they were taken to the woodshed.

Lilya kept expecting messages from her husband, but nothing came. The thought that she would never see Salikh again was becoming more and more certain every day. Now she had to take care of herself.

The first thing she did, owing to her family situation, was switch to evening courses. She had no intention of dropping her studies. During the day she took care of her daughter; then she pumped out her breast milk and left the bottles and the baby to the care of her mother. The mother was quiet for a time; then once, having had a drink, she started shouting at Lilka, calling her clumsy, dumbsy, not even knowing her husband's address, and failing to obtain alimony . . . let him support her . . . go to the university, find out everything from the professor "inside and out" . . . The next morning she put Salikh's things into two bags, all the while muttering in astonishment at what need there was for so many shirts— eleven! and three two-piece suits! These she took to the secondhand store on Blagoveshchensky Lane, where they gave her a good price for all of Salikh's clothes.

Lilya refused to go to the university. Vera Ivanna went to the Leninsky Hills herself. Having obnoxiously pushed past all the watchmen and receptionists, she found the Department of Mathematics and Mechanics and arrived at the dean's office. There she failed to find anything out, obtained no address, and was denied access to the professor, whose name she did not know anyway. Refusing to calm down, she undertook, in secret from Lilya, a second attempt to track down the runaway son-in-law—as she now was convinced he was. She found out the address of the Iraqi Embassy through the registry bureau. It took her a long time to get admitted. She finally wheedled her way in. They talked to her impolitely; they could not be bothered: just then there was either a revolution or some sort of a war in Iraq. Who cared about Salikh! Now Vera Ivanna finally understood that a strategic fiasco had occurred.

Recognizing her failure, Vera Ivanna decided to set things right. Having abandoned the attractive but unsuccessful project with a foreigner, she came down to earth and looked around. It would not be easy to set the girl up now that she had a baby. Then it occurred to her that this Arab daughter could be sent to the orphanage, where they take babies for five years and then either return them to the parents or keep them for good. She told that to Lilya. Lilya shrugged and said, "Really, Mom, you're quite . . ."

Then the thoughts of practical Vera Ivanna started working in a different direction: her husband Kolya had a nephew who had just finished his term of army service, came back, was going to study to be a policeman, but so far had been unable to pass the entrance exam. Maybe she should put them together? Vera Ivanna was pondering . . .

Lilya, too, was pondering. The girl Victoria was growing up, and there was no news from Salikh. And there wouldn't be, Lilya realized. She decided never to marry again. All her mother's efforts to set up her life were rejected . . . She studied English at school, and her mother came to hate this foreign language. Why couldn't she find a job as a ticket attendant in the Hermitage garden or in the kitchen of a diner—that would be more useful . . .

Lilya's life was hard: the baby was in a daycare nursery five times a week—a week there, then a week sick at home. She also could not find a suitable job: who would keep her if half the time she needed to stay home? The irrepressible Vera Ivanna kept dragging in some fellow every week, and Lilya responded by getting angry and snappy. Thus a year went by, then another . . .

And then Lilya had a strange dream. As if she is wearing white pumps, and she comes to a river, takes them off, sets them down neatly, side by side, and goes into the river. The water is warm and caressing, and she swims in it. In reality Lilya did not know how to swim. But in her dream she is so deft and cheerful and not really swimming, but as if flying in the light-blue transparent water. Then the water suddenly grows dark, churns up, the bank disappears from view, and she swims on, and waves her arms harder, simply leaping over the waves like some dolphin, and she is so happy—instead of being frightened. The most intense thought is, I'm swimming and I'm not afraid! At that Lilya woke up.

A year later Salikh had the same dream with small variations. In the dream he came to the bank of some water—a quiet river or a lake. Just near the water he saw Lilya's shoes neatly standing side by side. Lilya herself was nowhere to be seen. Salikh took his shoes off, too, and, next to her slightly worn white pumps, put his old shoes of his favorite "inspector" model. He took off his socks, rolled them into a ball, unhurriedly took off his clothes, folded his trousers neatly so that they would not get wrinkled. Slowly entered the water, walked till it reached his shoulders, and easily, unthinkingly began to swim.

In reality he did not know how to swim. But now he swam easily and cheerfully. Then the water grew turbid, dark, waves rose, first small, then bigger, and threatened to sweep over him. He struggled with all his might and swam out to the opposite bank. There was no doubt that it was the opposite bank. The one he had left was stony and his bare feet had slipped on it as he approached the water. This bank was sandy, soft. The astonishing thing was that there, on the bank, stood his shoes, and next to them—Lilya's . . .

Salikh did not make it to his father's funeral. He was arrested in the Baghdad airport and taken somewhere. It took him a while to understand where he was being taken. When he did understand, he knew that he was going to die. This was Abu Ghraib prison, from which few managed to get out alive. He did not know yet that just in those days the government army had begun to attack the mutinous Kurds. Poor Salikh, who always thought that owing to his highly intellectual profession as a mathematician he was above any political differences, wound up at the very center of the national cyclone. His family was one of the most respected and distinguished families in Sulaymaniyah . . .

Salikh was an Arab only in the eyes of his Moscow family. In fact he was a Kurd. But he did not see any sense in explaining the basic national differences to the Russians, especially since he himself did not attach any importance to them. An Arab or a Kurd, a Muslim or a Christian—none of it mattered to him . . . He was a mathematician, and the world for him was defined not by national or religious principles, but by one parameter only: whether his interlocutor was a mathematician or not.

His position in one of the most cruel prisons in the world was exceptional. He was in a solitary cell. They took away only his documents, and let him keep all his other papers. It was a five-star hotel compared to other cells. He tried to find out why he had been arrested, but the guard who brought him a bowl of rice and a tin of water once a day would not speak to him.

Someone else in his place would have lost his mind, but Salikh took out his notebook and began to write down in it his mathematical calculations, and his reflections about the relations between volumes and spaces, which existed only in the heads of mathematicians.

The year and a half he spent in solitary confinement remained in his memory as a period of the most fruitful workings of his thought, and for the rest of his life he kept going back to the scope and freedom of thinking that had opened to him in Abu Ghraib prison.

No one offered any accusations against him, he was not called to interrogations, nor was he tortured—something for which this prison was famous. He finally figured out why he was kept alive for so long. His uncle was one of the leaders of the Kurdish resistance. His surmise was correct: Saddam Hussein and Salikh's family spent long months negotiating for his life. He was, in fact, a hostage, but no one told him so.

Several days after he had that dream, he was taken out of his cell, driven to the airport, and put on a small plane without any identification marks. They did not hand him his passport. At first he was convinced that he was being sent to

Moscow. But he was mistaken. The plane landed in what he thought was Prague or some other East European city, then took off again and made a final landing in Luton airport, twenty-five miles from London . . .

Salikh never learned that his uncertain fate had been decided by an accidental phrase from a distant relation of Saddam Hussein, who told him that Salikh was the only Iraqi mathematician capable of becoming in time the pride of Iraq. . .

A year later the family was reunited. Lilya was issued a British visa, which the usually slow and awkward Salikh obtained for her. He met his family at Heathrow Airport. At the sight of his daughter, who had not even been born when he left Moscow, the father was deeply shaken. Plump arms, curly hair, little folds on her neck—and such a resemblance to him! For the first time in his life he felt a burst of love and tenderness, and little Victoria, whom Lilya had raised in strict restraint, responded to her father with unreasoning affection for the rest of her life.

By that time Salikh had defended his doctoral thesis and had a job in Nansen College. He was renting a small apartment not far from his work. The relations between Salikh and Lilya were better than ever: he was boundlessly grateful to her for the miracle of his life—the daughter Victoria.

The rest was the same as before. Only now Salikh did not send his shirts to the laundromat; Lilya herself laundered and ironed them, and also cooked rice ideally. After a week in London, she felt as if she had been born there. Now, however, she did not attend the language school, but accounting courses.

After nine months she "gave birth" to a certificate and very soon found a job as an accounting assistant in the college where Salikh taught.

Soon the family rented a bigger apartment. There were no courtyards by the buildings, and she now had her own room without a partition. At last she wore a blazer over a shirt and high-heeled shoes, just as she had planned in her youth. And she had as many pairs of shoes as she liked: white and black and a sort of reddish-brown . . . And instead of saying, *"My God, why should I care?"* in Russian, she said it in English.

Lilya never found out that early in the morning, on her way to work, Vera Ivanna used to take Salikh's letters out of the mailbox and hide them under a mattress. To give her daughter letters which she could not read was more than she could bear. The teacher of English at the school to whom Vera Ivanna came running with the first letter that arrived from London told her that she was not going to read other people's mail . . .

Meanwhile the war in Iraq went on, and there were also some sort of troubles in Russia, with Hungary or maybe with Czechoslovakia. Lilya never went back to Moscow. "Why should I care?" She had become a foreigner.

Blessed Are Those Who . . .

For Tanya Gorina

The elderly sisters Lydia and Nina came to the empty house in a forsaken Italian village by different routes, from different directions. One traveled by way of Milan, the other through Genoa. They had been invited by an Italian woman, Antonella, a disciple of their late mother, Alexandra Vikentyevna. Antonella lived in Genoa, where she was a university professor in the Slavic Department, and she had inherited this village house from her childless aunt. In the last ten years Alexandra Vikentyevna, a distinguished linguist and specialist in ancient texts, had spent a great deal of her time in this unoccupied house. Antonella urged the sisters to come and sort out the things left by their mother. Antonella did not venture to do it herself out of reverence for her teacher's memory.

Antonella brought the sisters to the house on the hill in her car, unlocked the little gate, led them to the house, opened the door, and left, telling them that she had to hurry to the university, but she would come back by seven and take them to dinner. She spoke very good Russian, except that it had an uncustomary but pleasing intonation.

The sisters remained alone together. They had last seen each other in a similar situation when, after their mother's funeral six months earlier, they had entered her Moscow apartment heaped with papers and books.

Now they were silently sitting on the terrace. The house stood on the crest of a hill, and looking from the street, it was impossible to tell that such an enormous, boundless view opened out from the terrace on the other side. It was a deep ravine, at the bottom of which ran a meandering stony track, the remnant of a dried-up river. The river used to flow down Beuca Hill, a spur of the Apennine range to the right, while lower to the left the Ligurian Sea flew open, studded with white sails, streaked with the foamy silver tracks of motor-boats, and marked off from the indifferent, pale-blue sky by the sharp, dark-blue horizon. In the closed space between the sea and the hills ran two roads—one far down along the sea, the other, a little higher, resting on enormous supports and heading into a tunnel. Slowly and noiselessly, trailers, trucks, and cars flowed along it.

The sisters did not know that these two highways followed the ancient Roman road that had turned into a pilgrimage way from southern France to Rome—the via Aurelia.

They were sitting, their eyes wandering, stunned by the enormity and beauty of the view, in a heavy silence, unaccustomed to expressing in words anything more complex than was called for by everyday needs.

"Beautiful," the older one said finally.

"Yes," the younger one nodded in agreement.

For many years the sisters had met only on September 1, their mother's birthday. On that day her small apartment, filled with dusty books, stacks of written paper, and cockroaches, was packed with many people—her colleagues, students, and former students. This was annoying. Why were these people so attached to her? She was a dry stick, didn't love anything besides the beetle-like letters of Oriental languages and the book trash amid which she spent her whole life, paying almost no attention to her two daughters. The girls grew up, one in the care of the grandmother, the other of hired nannies who changed frequently, allowing no time for them to become loved.

And what sort of family was it anyway? Sheer disaster. After Grandmother Varvara's death, no one held this female family together with little pies, or stays in summer cottages, or fussing over colds and sore throats with herbal infusions and buckwheat honey.

Even general women's conversation about life's little difficulties or cake recipes was totally foreign to Alexandra Vikentyevna. Although the men's topics—cars and politics—were of no interest to the learned lady either.

Having brought her two daughters into the world and given nature its due, Alexandra Vikentyevna seemed to have completely abandoned the female battlefield. She was learned. She herself liked to tell the old joke: a learned woman is like a guinea pig: neither a guinea, nor a pig . . . She was a learned being—wrote articles, books, gave talks at universities and conferences, was famous throughout the scholarly world, that special sector of humanity that was as wacky about letters as she herself was. She was even an academician in some foreign academies.

Normal men with appropriate sexual attributes never struck root in this family. The marriages of the older generations—Grandmother Varvara's and Alexandra Vikentyevna's own—were short-lived: the husbands were killed in wars. Alexandra Vikentyevna had lived with her husband a little over a year. The death notice came at the end of '41. She was barely twenty and her daughter Lida had just been born.

Many years later she lived through a devastating love affair. The affair was brief, its course stormy, its end stormy, and, by an oversight, the daughter Nina came into the world as a memorial of this none-too-happy romance. The appearance of a younger sister badly traumatized the older Lydia, who by then was almost eighteen, and the love affair of the elderly thirty-eight-year-old mother with a former student, who in terms of his age would have suited the daughter better, was unbearable and insulting. Lydia was never able to forget or rethink this fact of her mother's biography.

Lydia took the birth of the extramarital child as her own disgrace. She never managed to come to love her younger sister, the less so as she made an early and hasty marriage and went off to live with her husband.

As for the child Nina, somehow the image of the sister left no imprint on her memory. The grandmother did not leave any trace on it, either—she died when Nina was not yet one. Nina grew up with nannies who were rather regularly changed. It is with one of the nannies of the early period that the strongest experience of Nina's childhood was connected. The mother went on a business trip to a conference in Leningrad, leaving the three-year-old girl for a couple of days with a new nanny. This new nanny, a woman of dry intellectual appearance and with the highly suggestive name of Anna Arkadyevna, was totally unlike the previous country girls fleeing to the city from the life of collective farms. She turned out to be an alcoholic trying her best to overcome her addiction. The heroic resistance of this Anna Arkadyevna collapsed on the very first evening in the face of the bar chock-full of drinks brought and left unfinished by guests.

No one knows how the next three days passed. But having returned home early in the morning of the fourth day, Alexandra Vikentyevna discovered the intellectual nanny lying on the floor dead drunk in a puddle of drying liquid, and exhausted Nina, blue with screaming, sitting in her little bed in soiled underwear . . .

Those three days were stamped in her for long years after, maybe for the rest of her life: she did not trust anyone, was suspicious and very lonely.

While the younger sister experienced this three-day nightmare, the older one, who by then had a daughter of her own, went through a difficult breakup with her husband, who from light boozing parties with friends moved on to the phase of heavy Russian drinking.

Alexandra Vikentyevna refused to be distracted from her work by petty everyday problems: friends found her a new nanny, then she herself decided to send Ninochka to kindergarten, and, to support Lydia's crumbled life, gave her a monthly allowance.

In fact, the sisters were barely acquainted. Each thought that the other had the greater part of their mother's attention and love. With the years their mutual antipathy only grew, and on their mother's birthdays they seated themselves at different ends of the table, away from the center— that is, from Alexandra Vikentyevna, surrounded by a shield of admirers and disciples.

They had always been absolutely dissimilar: the big, broad-shouldered Lydia and the small Ninochka on spindly legs, with a sparrow-like face. The only thing they had in common was their loneliness, and the older sister's loneliness was exacerbated by the death of her dearly beloved only daughter, the fourteen-year-old Emmochka, of acute leukemia, which left the mother for the rest of her life in spiteful perplexity.

The death of their ninety-year-old mother changed nothing in the sisters' relationship. However, for the first time in their life they took a common decision: to dispense with the interference of the mother's countless admirers, who immediately and greedily demanded to be given all her papers . . .

Six months later they entered into the rights of inheritance—the apartment, the property, and the savings account with an unexpectedly significant sum. Here their intentions differed: Lydia would have liked to sell the living space left by their mother, and Nina thought that it would be better to let it and divide the monthly rent. For six months they conducted sluggish phone discussions, all the while being unable to decide what to do with all the paper trash the mother's apartment was tightly packed with. This total perplexity made them feel somewhat united for the first time.

Antonella's suggestion that they come to Italy distracted them from their burdensome apartment cares. However, having just now peeked into the Italian house, they instantly understood that here they were running into the same problem they had been unable to resolve in Moscow: the same piles of paper, the same dust.

There were no possessions, properly speaking: old slippers, a dressing gown, two silk summer dresses. Their mother had this quirk: she wore only silk—all other fabrics irritated her skin . . .

They were sitting at the big desk heaped with Italian books. On a reed placemat stood a cup with forever congealed coffee dregs, an opaque green vase with a vitrified flower, an antique table lamp unfit to be used for its intended purpose, and a small bowl with pebbles, shells, some cones of unknown plants, several Venetian beads, and a long-obsolete 200 lira coin.

It was terrifying to think of touching it all.

Their mother had left this house for the last time at the end of August 2009. She flew to Rome, gave a talk to the staff of the Biblical Institute, stunning all her listeners by her research into the last words of Christ: *Eli, Eli . . . sabachthani,* which she was convinced were spoken not in the Aramaic language, as everyone thought, but in a Galilean dialect which not everyone had understood and still did not understand. Then she gave the same talk to the Biblical Society in Moscow, after which she celebrated her last, ninetieth, birthday and two days later suddenly fell on the floor in her Moscow apartment and broke her hip. She was taken to Botkin Hospital, where a doctor of her acquaintance worked, but they refused to operate on her there and after keeping her for two weeks sent her home, a completely bedridden patient.

The sisters, prepared to take care of their mother, discovered that Alexandra Vikentyevna's admirers and disciples had already hired a round-the-clock nurse, as well as a cleaning woman, with whom Alexandra Vikentyevna had fierce fights each time she raised a damp rag above her desk. Besides the nurse, some colleagues came every day and sat with her, one could even say worked, and occasionally organized seminars at home, so that Lydia and Nina, slightly offended, withdrew themselves. They called every other day, asking whether she needed anything; the mother politely declined their help: everything was well with her. As always. All the places at their mother's side were occupied, and they were completely left out . . .

Nine months later, as Alexandra Vikentyevna's life was running its ideal course, she had a stroke and was taken to the same Botkin Hospital, where she died after several hours without regaining consciousness.

. . . It was a belated May, more like April. Several humble trees at the entrance to the funeral parlor were barely covered with little leaves. A huge crowd of people, come to take leave of Alexandra Vikentyevna, gathered in a big hall outside the closed door. There were even some foreigners, elderly ladies and gentlemen of ambassadorial appearance, one obvious pastor. Everyone crowded around a squat, unattractive man in spectacles who had become the head of the department after Alexandra Vikentyevna's retirement. The sisters huddled together, feeling themselves total outsiders.

The manager of the funeral parlor opened the door to the next room. There on the table was an open coffin, and next to it an old priest in a velvet skull cap was bustling—putting on a stole and cuffs. Two altar boys in black helped him to manage the golden harness.

The sisters exchanged glances: a believer? Mother was a believer?

People crowded around the coffin; there was not even enough space for everyone in the long room. The manager found the sisters and installed them at the head. Mother looked totally unlike herself: her face, puffy in the last few years, was now more taut, her nose had become narrow, aquiline—like never before, her lips were stretched in the semblance of a mocking smile. Her head was tightly wrapped in a black silk scarf, so big that it covered her whole body and no clothes could be seen—only the crossed, knotty hands lay over the black fabric . . .

There was a funeral service, then leave-taking, then the bus with the manager took the coffin away somewhere, and everybody went to a nearby café for a modest meal and loftily rapturous talk about the deceased woman . . . That was all.

The sisters left. Sat in a dark pass-through garden on the way to the Dynamo subway station, and for the first time in their life talked about what they had been keeping to themselves.

"She never loved me . . ."

"Nor me."

"She was a terrible mother."

"Not a mother at all."

"She didn't love anyone, only her little letters . . ."

"I took classes in accounting . . . It's numbers after all . . . I hated her little letters."

"Me, too. I chose to be a computer programmer. All my life I hated this education of hers."

"No, I can't say that. I was angry for many years, because she didn't give us a decent education. She couldn't be bothered with us. When I figured it out, it was too late."

"Yes. She ruined our lives . . ."

"Ruined? I don't know . . ."

With that they parted.

. . . Lydia moved the bowl with the shells and pebbles toward herself and began to finger them.

"It's strange that she collected them . . ."

"Yes, it's somehow . . . not like her . . ."

The second room was a small bedroom. The bed was carelessly made, as if the owner was not going to return soon. And the small desk was neat, not piled with papers. There were only several pages clipped together and over them some leaflet in Italian. On it was written: *Nostra Signora della Terza età.* It looked like some sort of prayer. It was followed by a Russian text, probably a translation.

"You think she really was a believer?" Nina asked her sister, studying the pages.

"Grandma Varvara certainly was. About our mother I don't know. She used to be a Party member . . . But then—this funeral service. She must have made the arrangements . . ."

Lydia put on her glasses. The handwriting was clear, without a slant, even somewhat like print—big straight letters, straight lines, the spacing between the lines and the words a bit too big, where an author's corrections could be beautifully accommodated. But there were no corrections; it was a clean text that looked final and even solemn.

She began to read . . .

Blessed are those who look at me with compassion . . .

"I think all those around her . . . looked at her simply with adoration," remarked Nina.

"It's not about her, Nina, it's simply some sort of prayer," Lida remarked and went on reading.

Blessed are those who adjust their steps to mine, weary
and slow.

"What steps?" Nina grumbled. "She spent nearly a year lying in bed."

"Don't you understand, she wrote it before she became bedridden . . ."

Blessed are those who speak loudly into my deaf ear . . .

Nina, who was fingering the pebbles and cones on the table, froze. Then she asked softly:

"Lida, she means herself, doesn't she? True, her hearing had been poor these last years."

Without raising her head, Lydia responded:

"No, of course, it's in general . . ." and went on reading ever more slowly:

Blessed are those who gently press my trembling hands . . .
Blessed are those who are interested in listening to my stories
about long-gone youth . . .

And she stopped:

"Nina, do you ever think about your childhood? Generally, what do we remember? I remember how I went to Crimea with Grandmother when I was little . . ."

"That was you . . . No one took me to Crimea. I was sent to the Pioneer camp."

"Right, Mama never took a vacation. Once they opened the border, she began to travel . . . to Rome, to Jerusalem . . . and she never told me about it."

"No one ever told me anything—neither Mama nor

you . . ." Nina shrugged. "What is it all about? What is it you're reading? What's it for?"

"Wait a minute, Nina. I see it now. She simply did the translation, it's something written by some Italians, see, it's written in Italian, and there are also ten points."

She went on reading more slowly:

Blessed are those who understand my craving for companion-ship . . .

"My God, what craving?" interrupted Nina. "She kept company with all those people only for business; all she cared about was herself, and she wasn't interested in anyone . . ."

"Stop talking, Nina, we don't really know that. She wasn't interested in us, not at all, but those others she did talk with . . . they always crowded around her . . . maybe in them she was . . ."

Blessed are those who give me their precious time . . .

"The more you read, the more it angers me: she never gave her precious time to us! Maybe Grandma gave hers to you! And when Grandma died, only the kindergarten gave me . . . its precious time."

Lida waved her away.

"Stop grumbling! You just don't understand: I'm already old, almost seventy, I understand it better."

Blessed are those who remember my loneliness . . .

"Lida! I can't listen to it! It's not about her at all, it's about you and me. It's we who owe our loneliness to her . . ."

"Don't be stupid, Nina! I left home when I was going on

nineteen, and you lived with her for many years, until we had to move to the Ostozhenka house. Don't interrupt!"

"But it's infuriating, Lida! Simply infuriating!"

"Listen, it's simply someone else's prayer, she didn't write it, she just translated . . ."

Blessed are those who are with me in the moments of my suffering . . .

"But she didn't want to see us." Unexpectedly to herself, Nina burst into tears. "She herself didn't want to!"

"We weren't there . . . that's true," Lida said softly. She was now reading slowly, as if spelling it out:

Blessed are those who gladden me in the last days of my life . . .
Blessed is the one who will hold my hand in the moment of my departure . . .

Lida carefully put the pages down where they had lain before, dropped her face into her big cupped hands. And wept . . .

"O Lord," Nina whispered, "this *is* about us . . ."

They wept, sitting at the small wooden carpenter's table.

"And who held her hand . . . we'll never know . . ."

"But you know her, she didn't need us . . ."

"Now I really don't know . . . why on earth she translated it into Russian . . . Maybe for us . . ."

"We'll never know."

Lida put her big heavy hand on Nina's frail shoulder.

"What have we done, Nina . . . Forgive me . . ."

"You forgive me, Lidochka."

They flew to Moscow, taking with them their mother's notebooks and the translation of the prayer of the third age that Antonella told them about—it was she who, during Alexandra Vikentyevna's last visit, had taken her to the San Donato Church where stood the sculpture of the Mother of God of Old People—Nostra Signora della Terza età. Maybe it was better to translate it that way—not "the third age," but "old people"? And there on the wall hung this prayer . . . They took along the china bowl with the shells, pebbles, and beads that had been sharing their mother's loneliness . . .

On the plane they raised the dividing armrest and Nina buried her frail shoulder and sparrow-like face in her sister's big, soft breast. And they both fell asleep. Loneliness had left them.

The Body of the Soul

Not a Single Lesson
Has Been Learned . . .

IN LIEU OF AN INTRODUCTION

The end of October. A boulevard. A bench.
To the east, framed by the hills, the port of Genoa,
to the west, if you squint well, the Côte d'Azur.
In your gray head you rummage through each fact,
which had been understood and perceived not
as it now should be.
Everything is false, askew, awry.
Cretin! Fool! I'm fucked!
Not a single lesson has been learned.
But what luck all the way, oh, what luck!
Not merited, just like that . . .
The intermission is over,
the third act is beginning.
Everything has been survived—
the first bruise and the last cancer,
everything has flowed away—
the honey from the comb,
the pus from the wound,
the Gospel, the Bible, the Qur'an,
even the peopleless Buddhist paradise.
I'm entering the final episode,
and whether it's sweet or sour matters not,
so long as it formulates the ultimate meaning.

I wished there were fractality, but no,
There is only frontality, as in these verses.
There's no poet onstage. But the hall is hushed.
The curtain falls. A black space.
Is someone there? Or nobody at all?

Slaughtered Souls

One could not say that Zhenya strove to keep up with the fashion; rather she caught the general drift and was slightly ahead of public taste. While all the progressive girls were hunting for high-heeled shoes, Zhenya bought in a second-hand store a pair of proper walking shoes of reddish-brown suede, on semitransparent rubber soles, without laces, with a coarse stitching around the top. The word *moccasin* was not known yet, and what wind had brought this American product of Indian inspiration to the Soviet secondhand store remained a mystery. But Zhenya was not looking for high heels that year, because she needed walking shoes to go to work. At the end of the year 1960, having fallen one point short of the passing grade on the entrance exams to the university, she took a job in a biology laboratory to acquire life and professional experience and, at the same time, to earn a track record that would be a strong point in becoming a student in the Biology Department in the future.

Zhenya liked working in the lab, and she very quickly mastered the microscope, the microtome, and the sparkling clean slides. The object of study in the lab was hormones, and this turned out to be like a fairy tale: during the day the tiny gland that was the object of their studies produced one hormone, during the night another, and this was determined by light, simply by the sunlight that comes through the window in the morning and gives the signal "stop" to melatonin and "go ahead" to serotonin! Most wonderful were the molecules: here they were, presented as a formula, and they could be synthesized. This science—biochemistry—was a wonder of wonders . . .

On a sloshy autumn day the head of the lab sent Zhenya to the meat factory to collect material for work—the pig gland called epiphysis. She drew the scheme of the brain, pointed with an arrow at how to get to this concealed gland by going up the stem of the brain and lifting the cerebellum and then going higher up and tearing the epiphysis out with tweezers. The epiphysis being an unpaired organ, it was impossible to confuse it with anything. Zhenya received a jar of formalin, rubber gloves, a scalpel, and tweezers, as well as a pass to enter the meat factory, which it was impossible to enter just like that from the street. She put on the new reddish-brown moccasins and went to the outskirts of Moscow, making two subway changes and then taking a bus. She was proud of such an important charge, but was also slightly worried about being able to accomplish it.

When she got off the bus, she caught a slight stench in the air, which increased as she approached the metal gate. She passed the checkpoint, and the watchwoman waved her fat arm in the direction of the processing shop—go there!

Further on no one asked her for any passes, and she entered an enormous space with a very high ceiling, totally peopleless, with a stock-still conveyor belt in the middle. She no longer noticed the foul smell, because human beings are like that—they quickly get used to everything.

Not far from the entrance rose a strange construction—a high wooden platform on which stood a man naked to the waist with a handkerchief tied around his head. He looked bored. There was no one to ask where the meat-cutting department was. While she was wondering where to go, some sort of metal parts creaked, an invisible machine began to work, and then she noticed that the rail in front of the man started to move. Before Zhenya could figure out what the strange mechanism was, a pig slid along the rail, hanging by its hind legs; and after it, with an interval of fifteen feet, a second, a third . . . The first one came up to the man, he thrust out his chest, assumed a ready pose, and here Zhenya noticed that he had an enormous hatchet in his hand. She already knew what was going to happen. In a quick, economic movement, he struck the pig in the throat, and a broad stream of blood gushed out. It poured down, at first in bursts, then in an even flow.

Zhenya deeply inhaled the foul air—and here stupefaction came over her. She was unable to exhale. Life came to a full stop. Her entire being refused to accept this horror. The shuddering pig moved on. Its front legs twitched in small spasms. Zhenya exhaled. Lowered her eyes. And saw a trough laid out below for collecting the pouring blood. Now the second pig arrived at the platform, and the man struck it just as quickly in the throat . . .

The picture was staggering in its precision and athletic quality, but also because the pigs did not produce any heart-rending noises. There were only the spasms of agony and the creaking of the unoiled mechanism.

She had to leave, but she was still unable to move. Yes, right—epiphysis . . . And Zhenya walked along the moving rail, where it was no longer pigs that hung, but only their carcasses, and she muttered to herself, "Slaughtered souls, slaughtered souls . . ." She was a philologically sensitive girl and during her last years in school had vacillated between philology and biology.

Now she heard new sounds—a clang and a hiss. The trough-shaped doors of the oven for singeing carcasses opened. The dirty gray dead body entered the oven, a tongue of blue flame flashed, and in a few moments something transparently pink, almost festive appeared and floated on, swaying on sturdy black hooks.

What followed was pure technology, which took place on the conveyor belt where the carcasses were turned horizontally and moved past women in smocks, each of whom performed a certain practical procedure—taking out of the opened body the digestive tract, the liver, the lungs, and the thus-lightened—what? wondered Zhenya, body, corpse, dead animal, or already meat?—former being moved further on, to that final point, which was Zhenya's working post.

She took her place by the table at the branch of the conveyor belt. Before her the pig heads, chopped in two, moved slowly. She put on the rubber gloves and concentrated. It turned out to be very easy to remove the epiphysis. From the moment she took out the first little pinkish sack, which still recently had produced soul-gladdening serotonin and somniferous melatonin, the magic of the work freed her from the bewilderment she had felt before. She quickly picked up the object of research with tweezers, deftly cut the delicate ligament that held it in place, and lowered it into a jar of formalin. Two hours later the jar was full. Zhenya sealed the jar, put it in her bag, crumpled the used rubber gloves to throw them out at the nearest garbage bin, and left.

Zhenya squelched up to her ankles through the stinking slosh that covered the floor of the processing shop. The suede moccasins of a rusty-brown color turned dark but did not get soaked through. Her eyes were searching for a trash can to throw out the terrible gloves, slimy with crushed brains, and she saw one almost by the exit. A bitten piece of fried meat lay on the floor next to the trash can. Thrown out . . . unfinished . . . One of the workmen had decided to have a bite to eat at work, cut off a piece of the tenderloin, fried it, but for some reason threw it out . . .

Zhenya got sick. She threw up very successfully, right into the opening of the can. Sour and bland. The morning oatmeal she was used to eating since childhood . . .

At the exit checkpoint she was searched. At first she did not even understand what was happening. Two men checked her bag, and then a woman invited her to step into a little room, took off her cape, lifted her sweater, and patted her all over her sides and stomach. This was her last ordeal of that short workday.

In fact that was all. The American moccasins were ruined; their joyful color of pine bark never returned, even after prolonged cleaning; they turned a dull brown. Zhenya never ate meat again. And somehow she did not become a biologist.

Aqua Allegoria

For Elena Kostiukovich

Sonya Solodova, a lean, middle-aged woman with clear, angry eyes, grasped the meaning of life after her divorce from her husband. The meaning turned out to be in food, or, rather, in the way of eating. But she discovered it gradually. Volodya suddenly up and left. After ten years of quiet, monotonous marriage, he collected his belongings, said he was leaving, and moved out. First Sonya lapsed into a tearless stupor, then she began to clean the apartment. She started by scrubbing the kitchen clean, so that there were no more traces of the grease constantly flying from the overheated frying pan in all directions. Volodya ate fried meat every day, and he especially liked pork. He fried it himself in hot butter in an old cast-iron pan. He would not allow Sonya to do it.

After two days of assiduous scouring, the smell of burnt meat was replaced by an abstract smell of detergent that had no relation to food . . . From the kitchen Sonya extended her cleaning to the entire one-and-a-half-room apartment. She cleaned thoroughly, driving out all traces of her husband and the smells connected to him. She threw out several books on metallurgy and a stack of instructions for some household appliances, and also his old shirts, which, though laundered, still kept the smell of tobacco and burnt meat. She even threw away his winter hat, which fell out of the wardrobe. "So that not a trace of you remains!" she not so much thought as manifested in her soul and body.

She passionately scrubbed every floorboard, she polished the windows, she got into all the corners. And having finished this total sanitary treatment, she sprayed half a flacon of the French perfume Aqua Allegoria that she had won in the New Year's lottery at work, when she still had a job. There was a smell of happiness and the wild guess that the promises, as if given in childhood and then taken away, had now begun to glimmer again and simply hovered in the air. This smell came to the apartment from outside and was akin to the Aqua Allegoria perfume.

The first week Sonya did not eat anything—she drank tea, munched on the long-stored apples from the garden plot of her cousin Nelya, and when she suddenly remembered that she had not eaten any real food for quite a while, she cooked some buckwheat kasha from the grain stored in the newly washed kitchen cabinet. When Sonya finished the last spoonful of the tasteless kasha, which she had even forgotten to salt, Nelya arrived, not empty-handed, but with apples and a homemade fruit bar.

The older Nelya's life was spent entirely on the six thousand square feet of a garden plot, transformed by her insane industriousness into a garden producing vegetables, fruit, herbs, and flowers, and a wretched shack containing a trove of food treasures. Her farming was extremely productive . . . The apple harvest was good that year, and Nelya had already filled the shelves with rows of identical bushels with labels identifying the year, as well as the name of the product and the number of the apple tree . . . There were four apple trees: three were Melba, with cheerful red streaks, and the fourth Antonovka, which ripened last, a beauty both outside and inside. The shelves were chock-full of good produce, but there was no end of apples, and Nelya shared the extras with Sonya and with her former superior, a decent woman of eastern origin.

They sat down to tea. Nelya told about her petty sufferings over apples, and Sonya did not say a word about the main event, her husband's leaving her. Portly and puckered Nelya cut a quarter of the fruit bar she had brought, put it on her plate, and made a habitual complaint:

"I see you lose weight without any dieting, Sonya. And I suffered all last year with this Dukan diet, lost six pounds, then spat on it and gained ten! No pastry, no candy, nothing but meat, all those proteins, so boring, and you spend the whole day thinking of something tasty to eat . . . But you're always skinny without any diet. What is it you eat?"

Sonya laughed: "All last week I ate your apples, and also cooked some kasha."

Sonya never had any thought about slenderness; she ate whatever was at hand, as long as there was no need to wait in line. She did not like fish, even felt squeamish about it. Everything greasy felt inedible—it was like eating the soil from a flowerpot or brown all-purpose soap. Meat had left her home of itself along with Volodya. Generally, her eating habits were not serious.

After Nelya left, Sonya realized that the air in the apartment was getting better not of itself, but from the apple presence. She also realized that no other food was necessary, that it was good the way it was. Out of a sense of duty she was finishing the store of grains, but she felt that kashas only spoil the joy and burden the body. Only the apples did not interfere with the happy lightness. When Nelya's apples were coming to an end, Sonya realized that she had no wish to go to the grocery store. There on the lower level, wine in bottles, dry goods, and all sorts of household objects were sold. All useless stuff. On the upper level were meat and fish. When she imagined those counters, she caught a whiff of the enemy's presence. And she did not go anywhere . . . She still had four apples left, and she sliced them thinly to last longer . . .

"How could I live so many years with all that meat?" Sonya wondered, and she was thinking at that moment of the meat that lay in the refrigerator only a few months ago, and not at all of the man who brought it home . . .

Sonya ate the apple slices bit by bit and for a long time. She was sitting in the kitchen, facing the window, in the place where Volodya used to sit, and her eyes delighted in the sight of the foliage that was bright and attractive just across from the windows of her third floor. True, this picture was now turning a bit yellow, and slightly bald.

Nelya came, bringing the fourth apples, as she put it— Antonovka. She brought two full shopping bags—ever since youth Nelya had been very strong; Sonya would not have been able to carry such weight. Sonya caressed the Antonovka apples with her slender fingers and gave her cousin their grandmother's garnet brooch. Nelya was pleased with such fairness: the grandmother was theirs in common, but the round garnet brooch had gone to her daughter, not to the son, and thus it was that Sonya got it, though Nelya bore the grandmother's last name, and the brooch, being a family treasure, should have gone to her. Happy Nelya left with the round brooch, the value of which, to her mind, was greatly exaggerated. Sonya inhaled the air and realized that the Antonovka smell intensified and even improved the almost evaporated smell of Aqua Allegoria.

The Antonovka apples, lying there wrapped in paper, were getting tinged with yellow. Inside they were filling with a slowly beautiful and dreamy taste. Some apples were still left when snow covered the ground outside, and, instead of birch greenery, the house across the street was glimpsed through bare branches. Sonya felt less and less hungry. She was sleepy. And thirsty. She did not drink water, but sipped through a straw the diluted apple juice also of Nelya's making. Nelya stinted on sugar, but she sterilized the jars so well that her juice did not go bad till the next spring. The neighbors' juice always fermented, but Nelya's—never.

Sonya's sleepiness did not go away. It must be from the smell, she thought, noticing that the air in her apartment was getting thicker, filling with the powerful, unearthly smell of solitary happiness, in which there was not a shadow of the need to share it with another human being. From deep inside her a thought would even emerge: it's good that I don't have a child, it would move around and befoul the air. She did not remember about Volodya at all.

Sonya made the bed with beautiful new sheets and lay in it. She would get up to pour more juice into the glass. She walked less and less. Occasionally she wondered what would happen when the juice in the jar came to an end . . . but it had not come to an end, there was even a little left, when something strange occurred: in those places where she had fine little hairs and a barely noticeable down growing, some colorless gossamer threads suddenly appeared, silky, pleasant, on her arms and on her legs, and she wrapped them around herself so that it all looked neat. She worked and worked with her legs and arms while she still had strength. She did not want to cut these soft threads off.

She had less and less strength, she had long ago lost the

wish to eat, and now even the juice lost its allure. Sleep was overcoming her. She slept more and more, and in the end fell asleep definitively. She lay there like a pupa, all wound in fine hairs of her own natural light brown color with a beautiful ashen tint. The apartment was filled with fragrance, which did not come from the Antonovka apples left in the box, but from Sonya herself. But she no longer felt it.

Cousin Nelya called her from time to time, but could not reach her. She took a long time to decide to go, and when she finally came, all her ringing at the door was in vain: Sonya was not at home. Nelya was even slightly miffed: if she had gone somewhere, she might have called. Cousins don't do that. But the bad thought crossed her mind and stayed.

The brown hair–wrapped pupa lay in Sonya's bed for forty days. Then it cracked from top to bottom and out of this hairy husk came a wet butterfly with bright green eyes composed of a multitude of facets. The butterfly sat drying for three long hours, then opened her now dried wings, and there was no one to admire it.

First its transparent wings began to flush with tender color. The scales were colorless, but by some mysterious law of optics the light from the window refracted so that they shone with a greenish-blue. Orange spots and streaks emerged in the upper part, and only an entomologist could have a clue that this enormous insect was related to an apple tortrix moth. The moth fluttered its four wings, rose, made a farewell circle under the low ceiling, and flew out through the open vent pane.

After another week, the alarmed Nelya came. She rang the doorbell for a long time, then tried the neighbors, who knew nothing about Sonya. One scruffy-looking old woman was surprised: hadn't she left for somewhere long ago? . . .

Nelya ran to the police. First a district officer came and knocked for a long time. He called the emergency service, who broke open the door. The corpse they expected to find was not discovered. The only living beings were flies that had had time to hatch in the apple rot of the last two Antonovka apples. There was a dark quivering cloud of them. That was all. On the bed lay some strange rags resembling woolen cast-offs.

The passport was in a handbag. There was a photo in it, and no other photos of Sophia Sergeevna Solodova were found in the apartment. A copy of the passport photo was included in the announcement of the vanished woman, and Sonya was put on the list of people lost that year. No one really looked for them, true, but the announcements were put up in the train stations and other populous places.

Sonya settled in an interesting place: moths like herself fluttered around her, and other butterflies, bigger and brighter. She recognized some of them. One was certainly her first schoolteacher Margarita Mikhailovna: she was big, resembled a tortoiseshell butterfly, and was flying solemnly and slowly without any light-minded fluttering. The air was light and mirthful, the fruity smell was strong and changing from apple to peach, from peach to strawberry.

There was no sign at all of any Kafkian insects.

Two Together

The door gave a high and drawn-out creak. Valentin Iva-novich waited for this sound in his sleep. Without opening his eyes, he already saw the whole of her—small, young, with a green ribbon in her pale red hair—and even sensed her smell: sweetish, with a slight whiff of sweat and pine-scented cologne. She used to say that her skin could not stand water, washed rarely, and preferred to wipe herself with cologne in the mornings.

Slowly, as if feeling her way, she walked toward his bed, and he, still with his eyes closed, sensed her approach. She was drawing upon him like a cloud, and he humbly waited for this cloud to cover him. With that the first part of their tryst, always identical, was over; after it came diversity, be-cause each time they met, something new emanated from her. He would not open his eyes, trying to guess what her first touch would be.

This time the tips of her fingers touched his earlobes, kneaded them a little, and plunged deeper into his ears. Bliss filled Valentin Ivanovich to the brim; he smiled and opened his eyes. She was lying there, light, almost weightless, her fingers in his ears, gently blowing "into the sweetie"—as she called the little depression under the breastbone.

He could not see her face, only her hair under the green

ribbon. He carefully pulled at the slippery silk, the ribbon slid off, and he sank his fingers into her tight springy curls. Even her hair was responsive. Valentin Ivanovich knew that the responsiveness of her body was ingenious and that each separate part of her body was able to speak: her childish, short-nailed fingers with his claws coarsened by age; her mouth, teeth, tongue, stomach, and everything deep inside conducted a conversation with his, and this conversation was delicious. Each time it began as if anew: first cautiously, uncertainly, then growing more animated, each time with some new information, communications, and this bodily whispering became ever more substantial. And ever less translatable into human language . . .

Their bodies had begun to speak even before they knew each other's names. At the time of their first acquaintance thirty years earlier, Valentin Ivanovich, already twice married, a lover of fresh relationships and an inveterate enemy of fidelity, habitually grabbed the new assistant in the lab entryway, expecting slight resistance and an easy victory. But his quite coarse grabbing met with no pretense of resistance. The response of her body was the beginning of that same conversation they had been ceaselessly conducting for thirty years now. And both of his wives, the first, Anastasia, an actress with catlike pretty looks and a successful career, and the second, Lena, his former student, later his assistant, intelligent, nearly irreproachable in all her actions, mother of his only son, and all his momentary women lost any attraction for him, although in the first year of this new affair he did not quite realize that his body and soul were destined for the monogamy he had despised since youth. He came to this realization gradually.

He knew more or less what was going to happen now:

first the whole surface of his body would come alive, would start to breathe, the whole of his skin would rejoice, every hair on his body would quiver in response to Gulya's touch.

Yes, Gulya was her name; in reality it was Aigul, a Tatar girl, but not from those dark, slant-eyed, and bow-legged steppe horsemen, but from those who, though called Tatars, come from the Urals and Altai, and are light-eyed, quick-footed . . .

For some time now Valentin Ivanovich had conducted this long conversation unhurriedly. In younger years the conclusion of the conversation was the most important part of the meeting between their bodies, but now Valentin Ivanovich no longer rushed; on the contrary, he lingered, knowing it all by heart and yet each time admiring the newness of what was happening.

The skin melted away, became permeable like wet paper, and it was as if the entire surface sank inside, and the conversation was conducted in an indescribable, a totally indescribable way. Gulya caressed his lungs, and his breathing met hers, catching the responding air current. It seemed to him that she even stroked his liver, its right lobe, causing a pleasant tickling, and his weary parenchyma livened up . . .

Her caresses were unhurried, thorough, and gave him bodily bliss and spiritual repose, the relieving of the burden he had been living with for the past three years. He moved to meet her and was already in her and she in him, and their embrace was tight and moist, and that feeling of mutual dissolving was already coming, when the boundary between bodies disappears completely; and as a sign of that utmost triumph of the flesh that renounces itself and gives itself completely to another being, when, to the throbbing of blood in the arteries, two purest currents gushed toward each other—one of the sacred, viscous fluid which contains the beginning of life, and the other—the water of greeting, invitation and acceptance.

Valentin Ivanovich clenched in his hand the crumpled green ribbon . . .

The clock shows half-past three. Emptiness. The sick-nurse will leave at eight-thirty. He has to have a little sleep. To get up overcoming a constant fatigue. To wash, to have some tea. To take over the shift.

He had long since learned everything the nurse could do so deftly: turning from side to side, changing the sheets without disturbing the lying body, taking off the wet Pamper and putting a fresh one on. She was light as a little girl, a dried-up bird with a sharp beak and faded remnants of reddish gray hair.

The bed was comfortable, accessible on both sides, but Valentin Ivanovich sat on a chair at his wife's feet, closed his eyes, and pictured this night in all details, in the whole sequence of intelligent and happy touches. And tried to recall everything Gulya was telling him.

A Man in a Mountainous Landscape

For Lika Nutkevich

His mother worked in factory management. Her position was called "Valentina"—meaning now be a messenger, now a cleaning woman, now run to buy groceries. She did not know how to do anything else, but her errand running was useful, otherwise she would not have been kept. Sometimes she simply sat and waited for orders from the actual secretary. Valentina had finished six grades; the seventh had proved too hard for her. She grew up in an orphanage, and was timorous and insolent. She did not have a husband. Nor a lover. Only a son, Tolik, and a room in a communal apartment.

Tolik stayed home. They did not keep him in the kindergarten, because he was frightened there, wept, and spoiled everybody's mood.

In the morning Valentina went to work and locked him in the room alone with his potty. At lunchtime their neighbor Semenovna came, unlocked the door, and gave him a bowl of soup. There was bread on the shelf, and he could eat as much as he wanted. He ate slowly and for a long time. The rest of the time he spent looking out the window. Till it turned dark. His mother let him out into the yard on Sundays, but he did not like these outings, he was afraid of other children. They laughed at him, teased him, sometimes beat him. He knew them all from the window of the third floor. Looking from above, he sometimes liked them—the way they played ball, or ran around, or stuck penknives into the ground.

Most of the time Tolik spent gazing at a lime tree with a big crow's nest in the fork between two thick branches right at the level of their third floor. The most interesting time began at the end of March, when the inhabitants of the nest, a pair of crows, came. This was the third year he had watched them. They first did some dancing in the air and then began to mend the nest, which had grown disheveled over the winter from wind and snow. They brought little twigs, poked at the nest with their beaks, flapped their wings. "They need hands," thought Tolik. "If they had hands it would be easier for them to mend the nest. But if they had hands, how would they fly?" Tolik squatted down, waved his arms the best he could. "No, without wings you can't fly. But hands are more useful," he reflected . . .

Having mended their nest, the crows began to hatch the young: the mother crow sat on the eggs, which could not be seen, but he knew that she would sit for a while and the young would hatch. The second crow fed the one who sat in the nest. This was the most interesting part, and he always waited for the moment when the second one came, landed on the edge of the nest, or sometimes just flew by, and passed the food from beak to beak. He looked out the window for hours, waiting for the moment, even the second, hoping not to miss it . . . Hup!—and she snatched it! Too bad he could not see what the food was that the father crow brought. Then the young ones hatched. He could not see them, except for their wide-open beaks, which rose out of the nest when the parents came flying with food. Tolik could not tear himself from the window, he watched as if it were a television screen. Now the babies get out of the nest; first they hop around on the nearby branches, then learn to fly, then they all leave.

Tolik was getting bored. He was no longer interested in the bird life he watched through the window frame. In winter he had another occupation; he was busy with splinters. It was only in the last year before he went to school that a radiator was installed in their room. Before that they had a wood stove and a supply of cut wood always lay by the stove. He chipped some splinters off and laid them out on the floor in some way—as little trains, or in a fan shape, or in some other whimsical pattern. His mother came home from work and was angry: again all this litter! And he cleared it away.

During the year before he went to school a small fire broke out in their communal apartment, in a closet that had formerly been a bathroom. Tolya slept through the whole thing. In the morning, when he came out to the kitchen to brush his teeth, there was a scandal going on—who is to blame and what is to be done? The guilty party was not determined, and the vote went to a short circuit. The inhabitants decided to raise money to clean and paint the closet . . . The objects that had not had time to burn but were just a little singed were taken to various rooms, and a neighbor helped Tolya's mother bring something like a trunk or a suitcase to their room—a box with handles. And his mother ran off to work.

Tolya opened the two latches with some difficulty, looked inside, and his soul trembled. He was looking at mysterious and exciting objects and dared not touch them. For the first two hours of acquaintance he only looked at the polished wooden racks with bright metal clamps. The color of the wood and the color of the metal reached out to each other, as if they were friends. The black, very black fabric on which these slender pieces of wood lay was also of an unfamiliar beauty: velvety, soft to look at. There was an object resembling a pan, but with a strange lid that had a round bump on top. Under the black fabric lay something no less mysterious but invisible. With a sense of violating some sacred taboo, of which his newborn soul could not know, but for some reason did know, he began to take out the objects that lay on top in order to see what was underneath. There were things there whose purpose Tolik was to learn years later: a photographic magnifier, dishes for rinsing photographs, round boxes with long-outdated film, and packs of equally outdated photo paper. At the bottom he found a small leather case which contained the best of all treasures: a plank with a frame on one side and on the other a little round window one could look through. He warily looked and saw in it his own window, which had long been the frame for his observing of life, and now this window was also framed. This object was called a viewfinder, but he learned that much later. "A looker-on," he said to himself . . . Had he been able to express what he felt in words, he would have said: life acquired meaning, and its meaning consisted in this very frame.

Three days later, when all the objects in the box had been thoroughly examined and the only thing lacking was the explanation of what all these wonders were for, the explanation came: the side pocket of the box had something like a lining or compartment he had not noticed before. When he did and opened it, he found many photographs glued onto thick cardboard, and he realized that all these delightful objects were necessary for making the photographs.

Each photograph portrayed one or several persons. There

were men, women, and children in inhabitual and incredible clothes, almost not humans but beings of a different race, like those animals he had seen in the zoo where his mother once took him: elephants or lizards or monkeys. These people's faces were serious, expressing solemnity and dignity—an officer whose cap lay on a special stand, or a little girl in a white dress and with popping eyes, or an old man with a little beard and a cane, and next to him a dignified old woman with a high coiffure of plaited hair on her big head.

Similar beings occasionally flashed in the television at his neighbor's, where he went in the evenings with his mother.

And he temporarily tore himself from his steel, wooden, and plastic objects and began to arrange the photographs on the floor in rows, in a fan pattern, or in some other order—by size, by inscriptions at the bottom or on the back . . .

The mystery of the precious box was partly explained when Mama mentioned in passing that before he was born she had worked for a lonely old photographer, and when he died in the hospital she had brought this box home, while all the other things were taken by his nasty neighbors when they learned that the old man was dead.

In September Tolya went to first grade. By the new year he occupied first place among the slow students. This way, being the last, he spent five years at the back of the class, having repeated only once, in the third grade. The teachers felt sorry for him and helped him along, and generally liked him, because he never bothered them in class or caused any pedagogical troubles, except for being a slow student. He was as if absent . . .

Once his classmate Zhenia suggested that they go together to the photography group in the Pioneers House on Leninsky Hills. This Zhenia had wanted to go there for a long time, but his parents refused to let him go by himself, and would agree only if he had company.

In the photo group Tolya very quickly grasped the purpose of all the objects in the box, and he could only regret that the main object, the camera, was not in it. But there was a camera in the photo group. Everybody took turns using it, and as a result they studied photography more theoretically than in practice. Some boys had their own cameras, but Tolik could only dream of having his own. But it is a good thing when a person has something to dream about.

He came to the group once a week, on Mondays. His classmate very quickly dropped out, but Tolik was ready to go there even every day. Here he ceased to be an ignorant failure. He followed every word of the instructor Kotov, and everything he heard and saw was fixed in his head as on a photo plate. Here he turned out to be the most quick-witted and skillful.

Meanwhile he finished the eighth grade. He was sixteen, and it was time to move on. He chose engineering school. Photography in his mind was a love and not a possible profession. But he failed the entrance exams and went to a vocational school. There he needed only to show the certificate of having finished eight grades. There were also advantages: a small stipend, and food coupons. By that time, true, they no longer provided a uniform, but Tolik was small and went on wearing his blue school uniform.

In the vocational school he was doing better than in grade school. He was no longer a failure, but solidly average, the same as everyone else, with the only difference that he had a hobby that distracted him from all the stupid adolescent amusements. He still frequented the photo group on Leninsky Hills, and was the most knowledgeable one there and very respected. And certainly the oldest and most honored—by then he had a diploma for taking part in the city contest "Love Your Country's Nature" and an award in the form of a plastic cup with a camera stamped on the side of it for second place in the All-Union school competition "My Native Country."

Of course Tolik was too old for this group, but Kotov did not drive him out, but kept him on as an assistant. Tolik mastered all the skills of a photographer—he never crumpled or tore the film when loading it into the developing tank; he learned to develop and print the photographs and give them deckle edges with a special cutter.

Occasionally Kotov gave him his old camera and he went off somewhere—to Sokolniki or Timiriazev Park—and took pictures of people strolling among the trees. He tried to fit both a person and a tree into the frame. This was not easy.

As soon as he finished school, he was called up for military service. Tolik was not afraid of the army: "I do as everyone does." On the eve of his departure, Kotov made him the present of a Smena-6 camera from the first series produced in 1960, which Kotov had long replaced with a more advanced one, but he was still sorry to part with the old one. Overcoming his natural stinginess and his acquired respect for the well-serving, time-honored object, he handed it to his best pupil. Tolik spent three months in training. He had never seen a rifle before, and yet he was the best rifleman in his whole group. But it never occurred to him that this skill was akin to the skill of a photographer.

For his success in shooting he was sent to the border forces. He spent almost two weeks on a train, with long stops, sometimes waiting at some forsaken railway stations for two days to be sent on, further and further to the south. He was brought to the city of Dushanbe. There eight new recruits were loaded into a new helicopter and flown to the place of service at the border outpost, hidden in the offspurs of Pamir, in a deserted glen, near the mountain river Panj. Through the small square window of the helicopter Tolya saw a world exceeding in its dimensions everything he had known so far. First there was an endless steppe, then the ground puckered up with hills, and this was the beginning of mountains lined up in long rows, of an unusual closeness to the sky, and clouds thick as ice cream. Tolya even thought he had died—there were no such things on earth . . . But the noise of the motor disrupted the heavenly picture with its crude throbbing. He looked out the window, mesmerized, until the helicopter landed.

After this voyage in the sky, the border outpost of Sari-Gor became the observation point of an enormous mountain world the existence of which he had never suspected.

The two and a half years of Tolya's border service were spent in deep regret that he had not brought his camera with him, and every day he mentally calculated where he could take a picture from, at what time of day, in what light, and at what angle. The horizon which the inhabitants of the flat earth were used to did not exist here; the edge of the world was jagged and irregular.

The service itself was monotonous; during this whole period precisely nothing happened: he saw no spies, no dangerous violators of the border. The main concern was catching smugglers with their inventive ways of trafficking drugs from Afghanistan. Afghans and Tajiks had walked in these mountains from time immemorial, transmitting the secrets of the trade from generation to generation. When they were occasionally caught, there would be some shooting . . . There was no sign of war yet in those years.

Having finished his service, Tolik returned home. His

mother was glad. If someone had asked whether they loved each other, they would have been surprised. In the orphanage where she had lived till the age of sixteen, Valentina had learned how to survive, but had not learned how to love, and she was unable to teach her son to love. She also had not managed to love any man. She remembered that in the sixth grade she had liked her teacher of physical education in his blue gym suit, but he did not even notice her. She yielded to another, whom she did not like, but who insisted very much, and then there were several similar cases. That was it for love. Valentina loved Tolik as she was able to, without thinking who his father was, and she did not know exactly who it was.

By the time of Tolik's return, a change had occurred in her life; she had been booted out of the factory, and she now worked in their house management office for the same eighty rubles. For her this was enough.

Nothing had changed in the house. Tolik rushed first thing to the desk drawer where he had left his camera. The camera was there. All his photo equipment was safe, his mother never touched it. The day after his arrival he went to Kotov. Kotov was glad:

"You've come just in time. I've been given money to hire a lab assistant. Do you want the job?"

Tolya did. Very much so. And he came to work the next day, although officially he was to start only in two weeks. This was his real homecoming, to developing and printing, to film and photo paper.

Again he went on his days off now to the Park of Culture, now to Sokolniki, now to the Silver Woods. He would have liked to combine human beings with nature, but the scale of human beings and the scale of nature refused to be combined. Occasionally, when people came to visit the trees, he succeeded in catching in the optic lens the mute contact of a man and a tree, of a man and a bush, of a man sleeping on the grass. It was as if the landscape diminished itself and did a kindness to a human being . . .

Kotov looked at his photos, grunted, hem-hemmed, from time to time praised. Said that printing in large format should be mastered, but there was no such equipment in the group.

Meanwhile a big event took place: the neighbor Semenovna died, the one who used to feed Tolik dinners, and her room—130 square feet—was given to Tolik's mother, frankly speaking, through a connection: it was not in vain that she had worked for the house management. It was the time when communal apartments still existed, but they stopped assigning rooms to new tenants. Semenovna's rotten chattels were dragged to the dump, and Tolya set up a photo lab in the room. Luckily one wall was adjacent to the kitchen, and he was able to have his own running water.

Now he worked in a new regime: he did not stay in the group from morning to night, but went there according to the schedule given him by Kotov—three times a week for about six hours. Kotov also put him in touch with the editors of *Nature* magazine, and he became their freelance photographer. He traveled on assignments, took landscape photos at the magazine's request, and occasionally did some photo reports in a laboratory or at the hunting agencies . . . Gradually he even began to read the magazine. In it he found all the material in chemistry, biology, and physics he had failed to acquire at school. In some whimsical way it all was connected with what he knew how to do—with photography . . .

He traveled a lot around the country—was sent to Buriatia, and to the Caspian Sea, and to Altai. He also visited Pamir, now with the camera. Usually he went out to shoot alone, like an experienced hunter for early game, and wandered about awaiting for a throb in his heart: here! I'm here! you're here! He spent a long time sizing up the surroundings, because he knew the evasive secret—a correctly set-up frame. And he clicked, clicked—more than anything in the world he loved landscape photography.

His photographs were pleasing; customers always welcomed them, occasionally they were taken for exhibitions, and now Kotov was proud of his pupil, just as before Tolya had been proud of his teacher.

Tolya now had more money. He saved for a new camera and bought a Zeiss Ikon Contax with a deluxe lens Biotar/2/58, and this was a life-changing event, like moving to another city, a marriage, or the birth of a child. His feeling for the new camera also involved a tinge of embarrassment before the old one, as before a first wife abandoned for the sake of a new young beauty. Although the second love did not cancel the first.

For Tolya this was the time of life when he stopped being a failure or a mediocrity and took a well-earned place among the professionals. And while he still lived with his mother, in the same communal apartment on Maroseika, ate the food that she never learned to cook, wore clothes till they turned into rags, bought new things only when necessary, nevertheless he had a whole collection of cameras. He needed nothing else. And no one else . . .

His almost wordless communication with his mother, with Kotov, and with several employers fully satisfied him. As in his younger years, he had not acquired any friends, male or female. He looked at women's faces attentively only in the viewfinder, and generally the most interesting things in his life took place precisely in this aperture.

From time to time Tolya took part in exhibitions. Once his works by some miracle wound up in France, though without him. But now he had good commissions: apart from *Nature* magazine, where they constantly published him, he was invited to take part in interesting projects, now something connected with the Exhibition of the Achievements of National Economy, now with theater. He won several prizes in various competitions.

Tolya loved to work on any new project. Once he worked with biologists, and took part in a bird study, photographing their habits, quarrels, loves, and deaths from cameras concealed in hidden places. He recalled that pair of crows he had been so taken with when he was little. Now the window of his room was on the other side; it looked not to the yard but to the street and was covered with dark curtains most of the time. On another occasion he was invited to a theater. This turned out to be quite a different kind of work; the birds interested him more, and the faces of the actors did not stir him as much as those he had seen on old photographs from a photoshop with the same address—Kreshchatik, Kiev. Now he knew in minute detail how those experts worked: the whole point, of course, was silver, which now had long gone out of use. In any case no one needed such quality now. The act of taking a picture, which used to be an event in itself, had grown petty and terribly simple. The proud and high-quality photographs of the beginning of the twentieth century had been replaced by dull amateur trash, produced in countless numbers.

Tolya's earnings were now substantial. He once asked whether his mother would like to quit her job, but she refused: "What am I going to do, cook soup for you? If you were married, I'd sit with the grandchildren . . ."

The question was posed at the right moment. He had just made the acquaintance of Lena, the dressmaker in the theater workshop, who seriously considered him as a candidate. She was a bit older than Tolya, and had a child, but Tolya was not troubled by the child and not even by the age, but by the fear of change—Lena was divorced, she lived in a distant suburb, and would certainly want to move to his apartment. But it looked as if none of the neighbors was going to die, and there was no hope for yet another vacated room. He even began to save money for building a cooperative apartment, but the saving process was very slow. Meanwhile fate smiled on Lena, and she up and married a widower with a big apartment. And Tolya's somewhat lame love affair dissolved of itself . . .

By the age of thirty, Tolik began to sense an as-yet unfamiliar fatigue—even the equipment felt too heavy for him. His mother, who ordinarily looked down at the floor or past his face, noticed that he did not look well. Something else was upsetting: he felt that his left hand had begun to tremble, there was some shakiness of movement and general insecurity. At first it seemed to Tolik that he had to bear with this affliction, that it would go away by itself, but the trembling of the left hand did not go away, and, moreover, six months later it spread to his right hand. This nasty trembling even began to show in his chin, and now not only his mother but other people began to notice it. Maybe it was, in fact, an illness?

He went to see the doctor only two years later, when his health was in total decay. His walking was now very uncertain, in small, short steps . . . Within himself he remarked on the unfairness of the illness: it could have been his stomach, or his head, even his legs, but this trembling prevented him from working, and he grieved, without complaining even to his mother, and sat in a stupor, assuming that his condition would go away, and he would go to the editorial office and get a new commission. So year after year went by. The pills that were prescribed did not help. The money he once saved for the apartment still held out. They lived modestly, as usual. He had incidental jobs, but it was more and more difficult to do them. He ceased to trust himself and his trembling hands.

He sat without going out for weeks on end. Occasionally he wanted to get up and go out, just for a stroll in Chistye Prudy. But then he would forget, would sit down at his desk in the room now unaccustomed to seeing him work. He dozed, woke up, fell asleep again. Before him were landscape photos. He kept looking at them . . .

His hands refused to obey him. He could not even hold a spoon in his fingers. His mother fed him now like a little child. Before going to work she put his shirt on him; he also asked her to put on his two-piece suit. And his ankle boots, too. He was unable to lace them; his mother did it for him. He kept thinking of going to the editorial office of *Nature,* but it never worked out: he had insomnia, could not fall asleep for a long time, trudged to the toilet several times during the night, and in the morning was drowsy, and fell asleep sitting on a chair all dressed and with his boots on. Waking up, he put his intention off for the next day, or else completely forgot about it.

Valentina showed great patience. She had it where others have love. Tolik, too, knew little about love, but gratitude, love's neighbor, was familiar to him. His patience was great, just like his mother's. He showed it in his illness—not complaining, not being angry, only surprised.

He spent hours looking at photographs of landscapes. All

that he had taken in the course of his life. Some of them published. But many unpublished. He spent hours studying the meandering path in the forest, pictured as if from below, so that it was not disappearing among the trees, but went up into the sky . . . Looked at the pictures of the sand dunes he had taken in Repetek, in the East Karakum desert. They resembled sea waves, only unlike sea waves they moved very, very slowly, and their movement could be noticed only by a fine veil of sand that poured off the top, sharp and curving slightly downward. One wanted to reach out and collect a handful of this very white rustling sand . . . And here is the slope in the Red Meadow where he had gone only five years ago on his last distant assignment. Or is it in Crimea? He took pictures then in the Karadag Reserve. After Pamir, the Crimean landscapes seemed old and worn. However, so it was . . .

Most of all he loved to look at the photos of Pamir. Pamir, incomparable to anything. The slope, gentle at first, further on became steeper, with a twist and a turn at the end, with radiantly chiseled mountains in the distance. Ah, to get there, to this white world, and walk to this turn, beyond which—he knew—was another, and then another . . . No, no, a landscape never allows humans to enter. Nature did not design it so that humans could trample on it, crush it with their feet, leaving the litter of their presence, of their impure breath . . .

But this path was familiar, a beaten track. It was at his border outpost. On this path he used to reach a solitary tree. Here it is in the photo. A mulberry tree. Then the road took an alluring turn, and another view opened from there, both expected and unexpected, as usual in the mountains . . .

His mental gaze reached the next turn. Amazingly, although Tolik had never taken a single picture there, he remembered everything . . . a rusty tin can . . . white horse's bones . . . a dented bucket . . . he kicked it and felt pain in his toes. He bent down, touched his toes. They were not wounded. But why was he barefoot? His fingers did not tremble anymore, but he did not even notice it. It did not matter.

Ahead towered the sharp peaks of the mountains, in the same order as they had been set up in the beginning of time: two next to each other, a gap, one big peak, four smaller ones . . . and beyond them another range, very high. And above it all stood the clouds, dense as ice cream, as if he saw them from above, from an airplane . . . No, this was not the Red Meadow, not the Caucasus, this, of course, was taken in Pamir . . .

Tolik walked lightly on this stony beaten path. The path was becoming ever steeper, and Tolik's walking ever lighter. The mountains were approaching quickly, as in a movie, and he already saw the ranges beyond, which could not be seen from the outpost. The landscape called him, and he felt that he would finally be able to enter it. The landscape accepted him. And, most strangely, there was no frame. There was no longer any need for it . . .

Valentina entered Tolya's room. He was not there. She called him just in case. Where could he be? His coat had long been hanging on the coat rack, and he would not have been able to take it—his arms would not reach so high. She walked down the narrow passage, where everything was cluttered with his dusty junk. Most astonishingly, on the chair lay his trousers, his old jacket, a buttoned shirt. Valentina picked the clothes up, shook them a little. An undershirt fell out of the shirt. Under the chair stood Tolya's ankle boots. Laced up. With a sock in each boot. One was darned.

Woof-Woof

At the end of 1944 Elena Mikhailovna, an employee of the Moscow subway system, received a gift from Lend-Lease. The line was long, she came late, and there was no egg powder, no tinned meat in a black-and-gold can, no chocolate, and she only got a child's toy from a big box with a picture of an eagle soaring over a boat. The toy turned out to be a little dog, even a puppy, made of dirtyish gray shaggy plush, with a short tail sticking up, ears hanging down, and button-like eyes. This dog was truly the smallest thing out of all Lend-Lease gifts, because the rest of the seventeen billion American dollars were spent on planes, Willys automobiles, and other equipment the Red Army needed. But her granddaughter Mila could not know that, and she was glad to have the dog. She was not yet two, but being a keen-witted girl, she grabbed the puppy, pressed it to her chest and said, "Woof-woof." This was the first name of the dog, who was to have a very long and happy life.

From the age of two to seventeen Mila fell asleep with Woof-Woof lying next to her on the pillow, and Mila whispering into the dog's ear all her woes and joys. Mostly her woes. Woof-Woof rendered its mistress this psychological help for many years, but having turned seventeen, Mila preferred to see next to her on the pillow not the totally sexless little dog but a being of the opposite sex, who in the line of comforting greatly exceeded the toy dog. At this point Woof-Woof moved to another room of their big apartment where Mila's cousins lived, who had just come to the age when children begin to be interested in toy dogs.

At first the twin boys, Petya and Pavlik, Elena Mikhailovna's grandsons, had violent quarrels over the dog—each of them wanted to play with it precisely when the other touched it. The dog acquired two new names at once: Pavlik called it Alma, and Petya called it Rex. Pavlik made it into a field doctor, put a paper ring on its paw with a red cross drawn on it, and crawled over the imaginary battlefield in search of wounded soldiers. Petya played a border guard, and he needed Rex to protect the border and to catch spies. He drew a wide chalk stripe on the floor and delighted in catching and walloping his brother whenever he crossed the chalk frontier . . .

The mother finally bought another dog, but Alma-Rex remained the bone of contention. The newly bought one was probably better, but for the brothers it was a matter of first love. Sometimes before going to bed they quarreled to the point of violent tears: each one absolutely wanted to fall asleep next to Alma-Rex. As we know, tears before sleep contribute to a quick dozing off.

When an interest in cars came to replace the attachment to soft toys, without any fuss they gave the double-named dog to Mila's daughter Sasha, who was the great-granddaughter of the late Elena Mikhailovna.

Mila looked at the now none-too-fresh little dog Woof-Woof, and ruefully thought that it had been twenty years since Grandma Elena Mikhailovna passed away, and her own not very old mother had died recently, but objects remain all but imperishable. After which she took the dog to the cleaners. Now it was a well-worn but clean little dog, and Mila's daughter Sasha gave it a new name—Kutya.

Mila smilingly watched Sasha whispering something to the new toy. Kutya performed her doggy duty properly: the new mistress dragged it around the apartment on a string, then began to take it out to the courtyard. And of course it became Sashenka's sleeping companion. It lay next to her on the pillow; the girl carefully tucked the blanket in on all sides and initiated Kutya into all her uncomplicated secrets. Besides, there was something particularly somniferous in touching plush, especially during weeks of illness. It was the little dog who first put its nose into potions and pills before Sasha swallowed them.

From the age of ten Sasha had asked, begged, and later demanded that she be given a live dog. Mila, a moderate enemy of house pets, finally surrendered. They bought a small gray poodle named Brom. He shat in the corners, gnawed on shoes, refused to come home after a walk, kept trying to break loose of the leash and run away. Brom detested Sasha's favorite game of dressing up, which Kutya tolerated so well: it was impossible to wrap him in a scarf or a shawl, or to put a hat on him. He might just bite! Once he bit off Kutya's eye, which greatly upset both Sasha and her mother, the more so as he swallowed the bitten-off eye irretrievably. On top of that, Brom claimed Kutya's place, jumped onto Sasha's bed, and whimpered when chased off of it. He caused a lot of trouble in the house, but a month later he got sick with distemper and, despite all the efforts to cure him, died, causing Sasha her first big grief . . . Pressing the reliable Kutya to herself, the almost adult girl wept over Brom. Now Kutya remained alone in the house, causing no trouble to anyone, not even potentially, since no distemper threatened it, and it patiently suffered any costume balls. In place of the bitten-off and lost eye, Sasha with her own hands sewed on—crookedly but solidly—a button that little resembled the eaten one. Now one of Kutya's eyes was American, made of glass, with a black pupil, and the other was pearly blue and slightly bigger. After this surgery Sasha loved her toy still more; it became still dearer to her heart.

At the age of twelve Sasha started going to the table-tennis club, to English lessons, and the swimming pool, and she no longer had any time for playing at home with toys. Although there were no more doll tea parties and dog dressings up, Kutya continued to live in Sasha's bed. It was not a young puppy anymore, but a being of quite an advanced age. It was nearing sixty when the new century arrived.

Sasha lived her life, finished high school, started at the university, and during her third year had a torrid love affair with a classmate. The little dog was tucked away in the mezzanine, next to Elena Mikhailovna's old astrakhan winter coat. Once again Kutya yielded its place on the pillow . . .

By that time the apartment had ceased to be familial-communal and became private. Mila's cousins built a co-operative apartment and moved out. Mila and her husband participated financially in this enterprise and received from the moved-out relatives, by way of compensation, their half of the dacha plot they had inherited together from Elena Mikhailovna. Mila was now the sole owner of six thousand square feet of land and a small two-room house . . .

To this little dacha, now free of relatives, Mila delivered all the junk accumulated over long years in their city apartment, all the old, no longer usable stuff she could not bring herself to throw out, being used to a none-too-rich life. Now

Sasha had everything—a private apartment, and a dacha, and a diploma from the Plekhanov Economic Institute. And she was married to that classmate who had once replaced Kutya.

The first summer, Sasha and her husband, Kirill, spent a whole month at the dacha, where they very enthusiastically began to set up their summer nest. Her Kirill turned out to be a handy fellow, and enjoyed this life-organizing. All the junk in three prediluvian plywood suitcases was transferred to the shed, the walls in the house were stripped of the old paper with its thrice-antiquated roses, and new paper was put up, with cheerful stripes and little birds. Kirill installed new electric wiring and even wired the shed. That was where the trouble occurred. When they returned to the city at the end of August, there was some work done in the village, and the electricity was disconnected. There was a short circuit, and fire broke out in the shed. Local people called the firemen, but by the time they came, the shed had completely burned down, with all the suitcases that had been kept in it. The dog Kutya met a quick, fiery death, along with Elena Mikhailovna's old fur coat and all the old junk.

Everything ended at that: the house did not suffer, and the fire did not reach the neighboring houses.

When Mila heard about the fire at the dacha she was very upset at first, but was comforted on learning that only the shed had burned down. She was even unable to recall what had been stored in it. She did not remember about the little dog.

The next summer Kirill finished renovating the dacha. In July a son, Andryusha, was born to the young couple. A fine blue-eyed baby. Everything was well about him, he nursed with appetite, gained weight nicely, his cheeks were becoming rounded, a funny wisp of off-white hair sprouted on his bald little head. By the time he was six months old, the color of his eyes began to change, as usually happens, from milky baby blue to the adult color that remains for life. It was then that an interesting particularity was discovered: Andryusha's one eye was growing darker and turned from blue to brown, like his father's, while the other remained baby blue. The parents were worried and turned to doctors. The eye doctor said that such a difference in color sometimes occurs and does not influence the vision. This phenomenon is called heterochromia. In all other respects the boy Andryusha was a healthy, cheerful child, gentle and good-natured . . .

By the time Andryusha was fifteen, everybody had gotten used to his different eyes, and they ceased to be the object of any particular interest. His mama, Sasha, a normal engineer with a normal Soviet worldview, divorced Kirill and fell under the influence of a samizdat friend. Together with him she immersed herself in the unknown space of Russian religious philosophy. She had already read much of it, when Daniil Andreyev's *The Rose of the World* fell into her hands. The author's life was astonishing; Sasha was moved by it. It turned out that there was much she did not know about the Russian historical process, which was so sleekly explained in all those Soviet social sciences.

In 1947 Andreyev had been arrested, charged under Article 58, and sentenced to twenty-five years in the camps. Part of his term he spent in a solitary cell of the Vladimirsky central prison for particularly dangerous criminals. He was allowed to write, and during this time he wrote many literary works which were a combination of bold thinking, powerful imagination, and harmless madness.

In his extremely amusing fairy tale *The Rose of the World,* his inspired imagination creates a world of various fantastic spiritual essences—igvas, witzraors, ryphras, welgas, and other raruggas. The result is a very particular kind of reading for lovers of esoteric philosophy.

This *Rose* sank deeply into Sasha's engineer soul and shook the rust-eaten premises of healthy Marxism-Leninism. Daniil Andreyev led Sasha onto a new and exciting path.

Among other things, Daniil Andreyev was granted knowledge of the origin of souls. This question had never interested Sasha before; she had not even known about the existence of such a question. Daniil Andreyev opened her eyes. After an insistent appeal to the Higher Powers to reveal the origin of souls in our world—whether they had been created by the Lord God at the same time, and were then sent down to our world as needed, or were being created constantly, along with each pregnancy, and descended to earth as needed, as soon as the newborn body uttered a first peep—the inquisitive prisoner received an ambiguous response from above: generally speaking, all souls (*monads* was the word he used) had been created simultaneously, enough and to spare for the whole term of the existence of mankind, but along with that, there exists also a tiny trickle of newly created monads by means of the accumulating and concentrating of love among people. For instance, if a child's love is intensely directed at some inanimate object—say, a toy dog—and this love is purposeful and powerful, then once the physical object is destroyed, the accumulated love concentrates to form a new monad, and it descends into our earthly world . . .

"Kutya! It's about our Kutya!" Sasha was delighted. And she was now perfectly convinced that the soul of her Andryusha, with his different-colored eyes, and the life of the plush dog of many names, the favorite toy of several generations of children, were tied into a mystical knot. Otherwise how explain his different eyes? And is it astonishing that by some sort of intuition they named their son Andrei? Was it not in memory of Andreyev?

The fact that the theory was not very plausible did not trouble Sasha at all.

The Autopsy

Kogan loved his atrocious work, especially those of his dead who left at the proper time—old, weary of life, bald, having lost lush growth in armpits and crotches, their well-worn feet knobbly and callused, their breasts and scrotums sagging. Slowly pulling on his chainmail gloves, he looked over a petrified body, an unread book, and formed a first superficial impression, evaluating the body according to a gauge known to him alone—whether the dead man had died at his allotted term or had failed to live to the limit set him by nature. Those who lived well beyond that limit he called "the forgotten" and was a little worried about himself joining their number. He did not like to dissect children and young women, preferring his reliable and lawful contingent.

Shortly before their divorce, Kogan's first wife, a gynecologist, said to him a phrase he never forgot: only a pathological type can choose the profession of pathoanatomist . . . Women's foolishness: a pathoanatomist, in Kogan's mind, was a priest of pure corporeality, the last caretaker of the temple abandoned by the soul. By contrast, his second wife, Ninochka, was a librarian and did not even know the word *autopsy*. And that was wonderful.

A careful autopsy usually took two hours. And during that time he was able to read the history of a person's life, as doctors read the history of an illness. Beyond the body of a feeble or slightly obese child splayed on a zinc table, his intelligent eye saw all the measles and scarlet fevers, the puberty crisis, the healed broken bones, the small traumas . . .

In most cases he confirmed the diagnosis of what led to death, but occasionally the open book of the dead body presented unexpected subjects: here was a fifty-year-old man who died of a heart attack but had an undiagnosed tumor of the digestive tract at the last stage. Or a famous actor killed in a car accident with blood vessels in such a state that the car accident delivered him from an impending, inevitable stroke. Or a woman suicide with undiagnosed leukemia . . . as if several illnesses competed in a still living body, and it was not always the strongest one that came out victorious.

Kogan was one of the oldest pathoanatomists and long retired, but from time to time he was invited to deal with particularly complicated cases of autopsies and forensic expertise. This time they called him on Friday, but he had already gone to his summer place and did not want to go back. It was his former student, now the chief physician of a big Moscow hospital, a whole medical town, who asked him to come on Monday, because the case was particularly disturbing, and it would be good if it were Kogan who examined it first, before the investigators arrived.

On the table lay a young man, lean, impeccably built, with yellowish-marble skin, a knife wound in the chest, multiple bruises on the facial part of the skull, abrasions on the forehead, and broken feet . . .

The morgue attendant, the old nurse Ivan Trofimovich, came up and lisped something unintelligible. Kogan had become hard of hearing lately and indistinct muttering to the side annoyed him. He grunted, the attendant nodded and turned the body so that part of the dead man's back could be seen: on both sides of the spine, from the third to fifth ribs, parallel to the dorsal part of the shoulder blades, yawned two strange incisions, which seemed to have been made after death. The attendant again mumbled something indistinct, and Kogan, touching the strange incision, barked:

"Speak louder, Ivan Trofimovich, I don't hear well. Has anyone touched the body?"

"No, they brought him like this on Friday . . . I'm surprised myself."

"All right, we'll sort it out," Kogan grunted, looked into the medical report, and wagged his head. The patient had been brought to the hospital by an ambulance on Friday at 22:45 and had died an hour later. The cause of death was most likely the knife wound . . .

Kogan looked at the laid-out instruments. A complete set: a scalpel, a saw, dissecting knives, a craniotome, a raspator . . . He began, as usual, with the skull.

Two hours later Kogan signed the report on the autopsy. Death had occurred as a result of a knife wound and the subsequent bleeding. The beating and the slight traumas of the skull, as well as the crushed feet, could not be the causes of death.

He came home depressed and completely exhausted, having firmly taken a decision—this was the last autopsy in his life . . . The two symmetrical cuts on the dead man's back would not leave his thoughts. His knowledge of human anatomy was perfect, but this was the first time in sixty years of practice that he had met with anything like those two pockets within these cuts, those elastic bags of unknown purpose.

He was a medical professional with a broad horizon and rational frame of mind, without any metaphysical deviations, but this dead man's anatomy directed his thoughts toward fantastic novels fashionable in the last century about extraterrestrials, alien visitors, or else toward textbooks in mythology for schoolchildren . . . He was confused and perplexed.

It was the second day that Marya Akimovna was sitting on a bench in the garden by the hospital. First she sat by the information window, and when it closed, she went outside and sat down on a garden bench.

Her son Vsevolod, Volechka, had left on Friday evening for a concert and had not come back. On Saturday morning his friend Misha, a pianist with whom Volya often performed, called and asked whether Vsevolod was home.

"I'm worried, Misha. He didn't come home, and he didn't warn me."

"I'll come right now," Misha replied.

An hour after the phone conversation, Misha, his nose disfigured and with a bruise over half his face, arrived at Marya Akimovna's on Delegatskaya Street.

"Yesterday, after the concert, we walked out. Some guys, also musicians, drove up on three motorcycles, very tough guys . . . They disliked us intensely. From long ago. First they grabbed Volya, tore the case out of his hands. He reached for the guy, but the other one drove his motorcycle over his feet, and he fell. At that point somebody hit me in the eye, and I fell down. I didn't see what happened next. Passersby must have called an ambulance. Where Nadya and Dasha were I don't know. I called them in the morning—no one took the phone . . . We should call now . . . now . . ."

And Misha began to call, trying to find out what hospital Volya had been taken to yesterday. Then Marya Akimovna called the church warden to tell him that she would not be able to come to the vigil because her son was in the hospital, and it would be good to invite Kirillovna or Zina to clean up in the evening. The warden was a stern woman, but she was nice, though condescending, with Marya Akimovna, and, having known her from long ago, called her Masha. Everybody except her son and his musician friends was condescending with Marya Akimovna, but she did not even notice.

They arrived at the hospital on Leninsky Prospekt between eleven and twelve. At the reception they were told that Volya had been transferred to the surgery section and that they had to go to the information window. At the information window a young woman with a bun and a bow looked into some papers and said, "Deceased." At first Marya Akimovna did not understand and asked how she could see her son . . .

"You can't. He's in the morgue. You'll be able to see him only after the autopsy," the woman in the window said. "You'll get his documents in the surgery section."

Misha, who understood what had happened before Marya Akimovna, seated her on the bench and burst into tears. Marya Akimovna sat next to him, looked straight ahead, and said nothing.

Her life collapsed, ended, and she realized that she had always known, anticipated, that this was how it would be. The picture of her whole life unfolded before her, from the very beginning. How her mama had died, how she had lived with her father, a stern and silent priest in the village of No-voselovo, went to school and was the last in her class. Then the village school was closed, and the children were sent to Ples, five miles away, and she could not go so far, because she was very small, weak, often sick, so she stayed home, and her father did not force her. She stayed home, stoked the stove, cooked soup and kasha, and when she grew up, her father's relative Uncle Osip came from Moscow. They talked for a long time—about her, she thought. And in the morning her father said that now she would live in the city, at Uncle Osip's. Her father left for the North, to Pskov, and became a monk there, and Masha had seen him only once since, when Volechka was born. At the time Uncle Osip, whom she had married on paper, because he was old and there was no other way that she could inherit his room, took her and Volechka to the monastery to see her father. Her father did not say a word to them, did not ask anything, but he baptized her little son under the name of Vsevolod, according to the church calendar.

The whole family returned to Moscow, to Delegatskaya Street, where they lived in their own room in a big communal flat. Masha and Volya were now officially registered in it. Soon Uncle Osip died. Masha took a job as cleaning woman at the nursery school. She and Volechka stayed there for three years, and then he was sent to kindergarten. And again she was lucky: there was a vacancy for a cleaning woman, she was accepted, and so it went smoothly later on: all her life she was together with her son, at school and in music school.

Volechka was an angel, not a child. He did not keep company with hooligans, but more with girls, both in kindergar-ten and at school. At the age of ten he made himself a reed pipe. He kept blowing in it, and tender sounds poured out. At school he was a poor student. He never finished his studies. Masha was not angry with him; she herself had not been so good at studies. She could read and write, but she had no use for the one or the other. Whenever she had free time, she knitted scarves and jackets. Also sweaters for Volya.

Everything went well: they had their room; her salary, though small, came every month. Volya studied at the Conservatory; they accepted him, although he had not studied in a music school. But the professors liked him; they said he had musical talent. Masha was taken as a cleaning woman there, too. She did her work very well—quietly, inconspicuously, cleanliness surrounded her somehow of itself. But Volya did not finish Conservatory. He could not pass the social subjects—history of the Party, scientific atheism, all sorts of political economy—and he accumulated so many "gaps" that they expelled him. He was immediately called up for the army, being of draft age. But he did not pass the medical examination—the commission found that he had tuberculosis. Marya Akimovna began to worry. The boy had always been in good health; what had happened? But a priest she knew said, Get him treated, pray, and trust in God. Doctors prescribed pills, he took them, got better. And he went to work in a woodworking shop. He liked it there. The workmen were all handicapped; they carved toys, spoons, bowls. Vsevolod learned to carve well. And he went on playing his flute. He played from scores, and sometimes his own music without a score. Masha loved it when he would stand in his corner, take the flute, and the flute would play now Haydn, now Mozart, now some very simple music Volya had composed himself, only three or four notes, but they were so modulated that it made you now weep, now smile . . .

It was then that Misha, his former classmate in the Conservatory, who had already finished the piano class, came to Vsevolod, and they began to play together; later other musicians joined them, Nadya the violinist and Dasha the cellist. They organized a quartet, began to perform. And Volechka became their head. He composed his own music. His flute kept weeping and smiling, and without him it was not as good. Still, he did not abandon his woodworking, because music did not provide them with any income. There were only unnecessary expenses. They wanted to record their music in a studio, but the recording did not sound very good. One could not hear the flute; the other instruments swamped its singing tone, and all the magic disappeared. Still people came to their concerts. Not so many of them, but those who came kept coming. And brought others like themselves, who found a particular joy in the old-fashioned sounds of the flute trills. This music was as if childlike and transparent.

Masha was the same as ever, only she aged and became Marya Akimovna, and she now did the cleaning not at school, and not at the Conservatory, but at the church on Tverskaya Street. They offered her a job at the candle stand, but she did not want to deal with money, she was not so good at counting, was afraid to make a mistake, or worse still—she could be easily cheated. And she got along very well with a rag and a bucket.

She knew, she had always known, that her boy was extraordinary, there was not a pennyworth of evil in him, everybody loved him. It was as if he did not see evil, and for a time evil did not look at him. But the girls did look at him, and many of them liked him. They would circle around him for a bit. There were not so many free men in our city, always more women. He never offended any of them, never promised anything, nor did he offer any male attention, and they withdrew from him one after another . . . Obviously each of them would have liked Vsevolod to marry her. But Marya Akimovna never talked with him about it . . . It was too bad, of course. Dasha was a nice girl, and Nadya, too . . .

So Marya Akimovna sat on the bench by the information window, without a single tear, and next to her Misha sat and wept. She was going over her past life and saw clearly that Volya had gone just as he had come, in a miraculous way. She did not know who had made her pregnant, where he came from, and did not know where he had gone now. One thing alone was horrible—why was he killed? Who did it? Who had a grudge against him?

Obviously Misha thought about the same thing, because he embraced her—she was small, and Misha tall, a head taller—and said:

"It's Volya's music, it's all because of the music. They couldn't stand it, it simply burned them. It's fiery, his music. Heavenly . . ."

"Yes, yes," Marya Akimovna nodded. She agreed that the music was heavenly. She tried to recall it, but could not. The music had gone along with him.

The pain was so enormous, astounding—greater than one could imagine. It was all located in the forehead, and he hung on it like a towel on a nail. The pain came to a point. It had a cone shape and was concentrated precisely in this point. There was nothing else left in the whole world besides the pain. Then suddenly a tiny shining dot appeared; it seemed to move, spinning slightly and drawing him to itself. The walls of the black cone grew still more black, and it became apparent that they were moving, as if this bright dot made them turn, pulling them into itself. He sensed the pull of this movement. The dot expanded, a sharp ray of light burst from it, and he headed toward it. The pain was with him, but it was also spinning and ceased to be so tormenting. In this expanding dot the note "la" emerged, and he adjusted himself to it and moved in the direction of the light. The corridor of the darkness spun, pressing him, but also expanded slightly, as if becoming larger, and his movement toward the bright dot was becoming ever more perceptible. He was being pulled there against his will, but his will was also directed there.

"Like a toilsome return home," flashed in his mind. The pressure of the black wall was weakening. He was already almost out into the ever-expanding light. But the pain returned, no longer as a cone piercing his forehead but now in his back—sharp and as if double. And then a powerful force pushed him out of the black tube, the pain in the back flared and went out. With a last effort he spread the big moist wings that had sprouted on his back.

His legs performed light movements as if he were swimming lazily, his arms were spread freely, the lifting power of the wings carried him upward, and he felt that all the dimensions had changed, the habitual grid system had collapsed, and the sound "la" expanded unimaginably, as if absorbing all the nuances of sound as well as all those that did not belong to the auditory span of a human ear . . . He was higher than the pain, it remained under his feet.

"They think they killed me. But that's impossible. It's impossible to kill anybody. Poor wicked children . . ." And now he saw with his side vision the tips of his new wings, semitransparent and iridescent. They did not have their own color; they reflected the radiance that spread around him, shimmering with pink and green, and it was as easy to work them as to drink or sing—just a little effort, like walking or swimming. And he swam, enjoying the movement, the gentle wind and the tingling light.

"But I didn't fulfill my task. Could I have fulfilled it? I'm not the first one to fail. How many were they, the immaculately born ones? One spoke and wasn't heard, another wrote and no one understood what he wrote, there was one who sang, and he, too, wasn't heard. And I played the flute . . . Where's my flute? That wretched fellow in the black leather jacket, did he take it? What a pity." But the flute—he suddenly realized it—was there! Tucked behind a wide belt that tightly girded his body. He pulled it out. A blockflute, wooden, warm, with seven holes in the front and an octave key in the back. He put it to his lips, blew. And it sang in the best of voices.

He was flying in an unfamiliar world, which was becoming familiar moment by moment, like a decalcomania, gleaming under the layer of swelling cheap paper. No, this world is not unfamiliar. We've been here, been here . . . He gave himself entirely to the movement, and to the melody, and to the elusive thought. This unuttered thought called him somewhere. And he floated to where it was sending him. There was no "in the beginning" and "then"—everything was happening simultaneously, and in all its fullness. "Ah, time is no more," he realized.

For many years now Kogan had not slept in the bedroom with his wife, but had made his bed in the study on a narrow couch. That evening he read for a long time, then wrote a letter to his son, who had lost his mind over some cabbalistic books. The son lived in Bnei Brak, a little town near Tel Aviv, and old Kogan kept trying to have at least a semblance of contact with him. Then he wrote a letter to his daughter, a professor in an American university. She taught contemporary psychology. From time to time she sent him references to her work, and he read her articles with disgust, and with the same feeling of protest his son's reflections evoked in him . . . He recalled today's autopsy. Those mysterious cuts along the shoulder blades were inexplicable; their inexplicability was irritating, it flew in the face of his strict and exact knowledge.

He looked at his watch—it was already past two. He went to the bathroom, took out his denture, put it in a glass of water, rinsed his mouth, urinated with some difficulty. Lay down and quickly fell asleep. But he soon woke up. Before him stood a hazily bright figure, unrecognizable yet familiar. Kogan stirred toward it, rose a little on his bed. Right, right, this was today's dead man. No words were pronounced. Only the soft sound, as if from behind the wall, of poor, bright music. A flute. The visitor was inviting Kogan to follow him. And Kogan did. There was not the slightest trace of mysticism in what was happening. A convincing reality . . .

In the morning his wife twice called him to come and have breakfast. He did not come. She went into his study. The dead Kogan lay under a checkered plaid, smiling.

A Serpentine Road

To the memory of Katya Genieva

Nadezhda Georgievna had worked as a bibliographer since ancient, pre-computer days. When computers appeared in the life of her generation, she was the first to admire the cleverness of the new device and felt to the bottom of her heart that the world had changed enormously and irrevocably. And she was the first in the whole huge library to master all this new wisdom.

Library workers, surrounded by old books and dated news, are—by their protective nature—conservative folk, resisting any, even the most insignificant, innovations, like transferring the box of catalogue cards from one corner of a storeroom to another. Then, at the beginning of the computer age, a deep divide emerged, which some people stepped over—easily or with great difficulty—while others accepted that they would forever remain in the world where bibliographic cards covered with neat handwriting are securely impaled on a metal rod. They had on them everything that was necessary: the title of the book, the name of the author, the publisher's imprint.

Nadezhda Georgievna, far from the youngest of the library workers, made the leap into the new millennium quite painlessly. Neither her daughter Lida nor her son Misha showed such agility. Yet no one was particularly surprised at her achievements, because everyone around knew that her memory was boundless and her character had the power of a steam engine.

Anticipating her future success, Nadezhda Georgievna began the total reorganization of the library in a new way. The oldest colleagues, feeling professional inferiority, hastened to take their retirement, and the new girls, who came to replace them after library courses or even university, were all goofy and daffy, and so Nadezhda Georgievna organized an almost underground team of bold hopefuls and began to teach them the new computer science.

Some grasped everything on the fly, at one stroke—and those who could not changed profession. Incidentally, often to a much more lucrative one. Everyone knows that in all times, in libraries Babylonian or Alexandrian, a special breed of people work who believe in books as others believe in the Lord God.

Nadezhda Georgievna, who had already gone beyond the age of retirement, belonged to this breed of book worshippers and had no intention of leaving her work. Because first, and second, and third . . .

All these numerous reasons were presented to her daughter Lida, who was unable to cope with her belatedly born twins and dreamed of living with her mother and having her babysit the grandchildren . . . But Nadezhda Georgievna would not even hear of it: children, as we all know, grow by themselves, and the book business needed care, especially in this period crucial for the life of libraries.

She held enormous plans in her head, and, having begun something, never stopped until she brought it to a triumphant end. And there was another astonishing feature in her behavior: she spoke both with her superiors and with her subordinates with the same intonation of friendly sympathy, in which there was no superiority toward those below nor special, respectful ingratiation toward those above . . . She omitted nothing, forgot nothing, not even the name of the cleaning woman's granddaughter.

Nadezhda Georgievna was a little under sixty when she forgot the word *serpentine*. She was telling a friend about her childhood in a village near Gagry, and describing what a beautiful steep path used to lead up the hill to her grandmother's house, and how later this path got overgrown, because a road was laid up that steep hill, a kind of . . . here she stumbled. The word *serpentine* left her mind, and in its place yawned a distinct emptiness. A blank . . . a white spot.

Unruffled, she drew a zigzag in the air with her fingers. And zigzagged the conversation in a different direction, a culinary one, and told what a tasty pie her grandmother had baked during the hungry years practically out of the grass under their feet . . . all the while searching for the vanished word at the bottom of her memory, in order to fill up this blank. And then she suddenly realized that it was not the first time this had happened to her—this lapsing of a word. Yes, recently she had tried to remember her school friend's phone number and could not. Yet all her life she had remembered all phone numbers by heart, like the "Our Father." She just lost them.

She was confused, perplexed, nervous. Maybe just overtired?

The word *serpentine* came back the next day as if nothing had happened. But it turned out to be only the first bell. The next day she could not remember the title of McEwan's novel that she liked so much . . .

She was losing words, names, numbers. Words and numbers—nothing. It was worse—she noticed that going to the kitchen to get a glass of water, she would forget why she was going, return to where she had been in order to remember, and then go again . . .

Those multiple trips to get a cup, a plate, a towel. She lost her passport . . . though she found it a bit later. She needed the passport very much just then for getting a working visa for Germany. The matter was of great importance, not a pointless promenade for the beauty of it: she had to return to a museum in Leipzig the books taken from it during the war.

She would stop more and more often in a momentary stupor, trying to restore the sequence of actions she used to perform automatically. No one noticed it except herself. She did not even have anyone with whom she could share her trouble, concealed so far. More acute grew the uneasiness about forgetting something important and urgent at work.

She began to write little notices for herself—Don't forget. This or that person to call, to meet. Separate ones to remember what to buy in the supermarket. And then forgot where she put the list . . .

One day, when her daughter came to see her with the grandchildren, she forgot the name of one of them. When they were gone, Nadezhda Georgievna remembered the boy's name—Maxim! And wept . . . She realized that she was suffering from a disgusting and shameful illness.

Nadezhda Georgievna called it "the serpentine illness" and was quite successful in concealing it from the people around her. After six months it was clear that she was losing even the names of her colleagues, and she learned to fill the resulting pauses with all sorts of impersonal words like "my dear," "dear heart," "my friend" . . .

Being already used to getting all answers to all questions

from the internet, Nadezhda Georgievna looked up "deterioration of memory and how to fight it." Information poured out in torrents. The research demonstrated that cognitive destruction occurs, which leads to the malfunction of operative memory. Treatments were suggested: promenades, vitamin B12, some special sort of apple in mild cases; for more serious cases—medications from glycine to Nootropyl, plus a whole heap of other things.

She bought it all, wrote down on a scrap of paper what to take and how to take it. Three copies. One by the bed, another in the kitchen, the third in the entryway, by the door ... It seemed to help, she thought. But—strangely!—words kept escaping, getting lost, and when she concentrated on trying to catch the fugitives, instead of the Russian words she recalled the same words in German or in English. For some reason her native Russian turned out to be the most volatile, and the wind of oblivion blew away precisely the Russian words. Instead arrived words in German, the first foreign language she had been taught in childhood by her mother: *Die Deutsche Sprache ... Ich erinnere mich ... kleines Mädchen ...* or some useless English ones: *keep silence, you crazy guy ... I can't help you, my honey ... serpentine ...*

This cursed forgetfulness began with a breakfast she could skip, thinking she had already had it, or would have a second time, forgetting that she had just eaten it. The knowledge of what happened just now, a day or a week before, dissolved, but the further back from the present day the memory was, the firmer it held.

Nadezhda Georgievna took a vacation from work. She had vacation time saved up from the last three years.

Her son Misha came. She could not recall when she had last seen him.

"Why haven't you been to see me for so long?" she asked him.

"But, Mom, I was here two days ago."

Then she told him that she had troubles with her memory, that she kept forgetting everything . . . Misha was a very busy man, overloaded with his own work, but he instantly realized that he had to pick up and carry, and that he did.

He was as far from medicine as from the sky. All his affairs were very down to earth. At the time he was dealing in some building lots near Moscow, built cottages, bought, sold, resold. And he immediately busied himself with his mother with the same clarity and consistency that was inherent in him. Maybe it was from her that he took it . . .

He sent her to see all the renowned and expensive doctors, first the generalists and neurologists, who prescribed to her the same pills she had dug up on the internet and gave her some infusions, but nothing helped. She was getting worse. Then Misha made a second go at it—homeopaths, Chinese doctors with cauterizations and acupunctures, a real Tibetan herbalist, who worked with an interpreter. Misha's wife, Svetlana, inclined to folk mysticism, brought Nadezhda Georgievna a famous sorceress in a man's fur hat who boiled some water in a dirty pot she had with her, put some magic trash in it, looked for a long time at the bubbling scraps of some roots, waited till the water cooled, mixed it with some oil, smeared Nadezhda Georgievna's ears, nose, and mouth with it, and had her drink the rest . . . Some sort of swill.

When the old woman left, Nadezhda Georgievna went to the bathroom, washed the magic potion off, and said, "That's it, children . . . *Genug* . . . *finita la commedia* . . . Enough."

This was probably the last decision of her life.

Her world was shrinking, the blank spots of escaped and forgotten things expanded, the names of people, the titles of books, the memories disappeared—not only the memories from yesterday but also the precious notches from childhood: how she was bitten by a dog in the yard, how she spilled ink on a white school pinafore, how in the sixth grade she broke her leg at the exam for the badge in physical and patriotic fitness. She forgot her mother, father, husband . . . Everything abstract, speculative, obtained in the course of life through reading, learning, contacts with people dissolved. All the immense library of knowledge that she valued so much. As if her thoughts were descending from a height into a hollow: where is the boiling kettle—she forgot, the water boiled away . . . the blackened kettle . . . her son brought an electric one . . . here's the switch, the light goes on . . .

Her daughter Lida came. Nadezhda Georgievna gave her a friendly smile, nodded, and asked, "How are you doing, dear miss?" Lida burst into tears.

Her son arranged for Nadezhda Georgievna to stay in a special, very expensive old people's home in a Moscow suburb . . . It was comfortable there, she calmed down, the loss of words no longer made her suffer, partly because they abandoned her completely and no longer vexed her with a temporary absence, partly because she was given injections of special calmative and restorative drugs which made her sleep most of the time. Occasionally she got up, seated herself by the window in her beautiful mauve house robe, and looked out. The calming snowy blankness outside merged with the blankness inside her, which used to torment her so much. Now her inner emptiness was total, whereas before it had been spotty, chaotic, with a struggle for little islands tinged with love, anxiety, desire for action—there had been movement in it, as in a children's game . . . the game of . . . no, she forgot its name. The present blankness was not anxious, not menacing as in an operating room, but of a totally different kind—calming, gentle, reassuring. On a par with the thick and heavy blanket of snow opening outside the window . . .

That morning Nadezhda Georgievna, with the help of a nurse, ate some oatmeal and cottage cheese, drank coffee with milk, as she always did in the morning, and then for a long time sat before the window, given to the sense of blankness inside and outside, without beginning or end . . . She sat in benumbed concentration until the moment when this immobile blankness was torn open by a cluster of blue lightnings, one of which struck her head. The stroke broke into this calming blankness; with a high ringing it split and turned out to be only a curtain. And the curtain fell.

Nadezhda Georgievna cried out. The picture that opened before her was much bigger than the world she lived in. There were no blank or empty spaces—the thick and beautiful fabric was the cosmos in which the earth and everything living on it and all the knowledge of plants, microbes, ants, elephants, and people were gathered together and communicated by flowing into each other. This was complete knowledge, perfect and constantly increasing.

All her life she had been reading books, filling in catalogue cards, and wondering at the huge amount of varied knowledge in the world, diverse and disjointed. When computers came, it turned out that the boundaries of the known extended much further than she had been thinking. And she was learning to tread the new paths . . .

But here was a world not of learning but of perfect knowledge, and it had no boundaries . . . Everything she knew from books—from the school grammar to the anthology of the ancient world, from the proof of the Pythagorean theorem to the structure of phloem—was only a small part of the space that opened to her.

. . . This intelligent chaos was beckoning to her, it needed her.

"Where are my glasses?" flashed the thought. But she realized at once that her vision was excellent and that now she saw everything in a different way from before, as if not in the habitual three-dimensional way, but somehow differently. This was the great beauty she had anticipated sitting in her library, in the department of new arrivals, but she never thought, never hoped she would see herself in this place, and happiness filled her to the brim, to the point of losing her own boundaries. She felt that she had been accepted here forever, and what she loved most of all in her life—studying, learning the new, and expanding this knowledge to the furthermost points her ailing, overcharged, work-weary consciousness could embrace—all of it was given her at once and forever. This radiant world had no boundaries. It moved, developed, expanded, and unfolded like a serpentine road . . .

LUDMILA ULITSKAYA (b. 1943) is an internationally acclaimed Russian novelist and short story writer. She was born in the Ural Mountains in western Russia and began her career as a scientist at the Institute of Genetics. Shortly before perestroika, she began her literary career as a scriptwriter and repertory director of the Hebrew Theatre of Moscow, and she began publishing short fiction and novels in 1990. Many of her novels have been translated into English, including *Jacob's Ladder, The Big Green Tent, Daniel Stein, Interpreter,* and *The Funeral Party.* She is the author of numerous collections of short stories for both adults and children, the playwright of six productions staged in Russia and throughout Europe, and the recipient of many national and international awards, including the Prix Formentor in 2022. She is widely acclaimed as one of the most profound and far-reaching contemporary Russian authors.

RICHARD PEVEAR and LARISSA VOLOKHONSKY have translated *Novels, Tales, Journeys* by Alexander Pushkin; Nikolai Gogol's *Dead Souls* and *Collected Tales;* the major works of Fyodor Dostoyevsky and Leo Tolstoy; *The Enchanted Wanderer and Other Stories* by Nikolai Leskov; three collections of stories and short novels by Anton Chekhov as well as a number of his plays (in collaboration with the playwright Richard Nelson); *The Master and Margarita* by Mikhail Bulgakov; and Boris Pasternak's *Doctor Zhivago.* Their translations of *The Brothers Karamazov* and *Anna Karenina* were awarded the PEN Book-of-the-Month Club translation prize. In 2006 they received the first Efim Etkind Translation Prize from the European University of Saint Petersburg.

RICHARD PEVEAR was born in Waltham, Massachusetts. He has published translations of works by Alain, Yves Bonnefoy, Alberto Savinio, Pavel Florensky, and Henri Volokhonsky. He has received fellowships or grants for translation from the National Endowment for the Arts, the Ingram Merrill Foundation, the Guggenheim Foundation, the National Endowment for the Humanities, and the French Ministry of Culture.

LARISSA VOLOKHONSKY was born in Leningrad and graduated from Leningrad State University with an M.A. in linguistics. She has translated works by the prominent Orthodox theologians Alexander Schmemann and John Meyendorff into Russian, and is now working on a Russian translation of stories by Isak Dinesen.